Niwi

A VOICE IN THE NIGHT

Also by Andrea Camilleri

Inspector Montalbano mysteries

THE SHAPE OF WATER

THE TERRACOTTA DOG

THE SNACK THIEF

THE VOICE OF THE VIOLIN

EXCURSION TO TINDARI

THE SCENT OF THE NIGHT

ROUNDING THE MARK

THE PATIENCE OF THE SPIDER

THE PAPER MOON

AUGUST HEAT

THE WINGS OF THE SPHINX

THE TRACK OF SAND

THE POTTER'S FIELD

THE AGE OF DOUBT

THE DANCE OF THE SEAGULL

THE TREASURE HUNT

ANGELICA'S SMILE

GAME OF MIRRORS

BLADE OF LIGHT

Short stories

MONTALBANO'S FIRST CASE AND OTHER STORIES

Other novels

HUNTING SEASON

THE BREWER OF PRESTON

ANDREA CAMILLERI

A VOICE IN THE NIGHT

Translated by Stephen Sartarelli

MANTLE

First published 2016 by Penguin Books,
an imprint of Penguin Random House LLC

First published in the UK 2016 by Mantle
an imprint of Pan Macmillan
20 New Wharf Road, London N1 9RR
Associated companies throughout the world
www.panmacmillan.com

ISBN 978-1-4472-6456-9

Originally published in Italian 2012 as *Una voce di notte* by Sellerio Editore, Palermo

1 3 5 7 9 8 6 4 2

A CIP catalogue record for this book is available from the British Library.

Typeset by Ellipsis Digital Limited, Glasgow
Printed and bound by CPI Group (UK) Ltd, Croydon, CR0 4YY

Visit **www.panmacmillan.com** to read more about all our books
and to buy them. You will also find features, author interviews and
news of any author events, and you can sign up for e-newsletters
so that you're always first to hear about our new releases.

A VOICE IN THE NIGHT

ONE

He woke up at exactly six-thirty a.m., rested, fresh, and perfectly lucid.

He got up, went and opened the shutters, and looked outside.

Calm sea, flat as a table, and a clear sky, blue with a few small white clouds, that looked as if it had been painted by a Sunday painter and put there as decoration. A decidedly anonymous day, but he liked it precisely because of its lack of character.

For there are certain days that from the first light of dawn impose their strong personalities on you, and you have no choice but to bend down, submit, and put up.

He went back to bed. There was nothing to do at the office, and so he might as well take it easy.

Had he dreamed?

He'd read in a magazine that one always dreams, and that even when we think we haven't, it's because in waking up we forget what we've dreamed.

And perhaps this loss of dream memory was also due to age. In fact, at one point in his life, the moment he opened his eyes his dreams of the night would come rushing back to him and he could watch them unfold in sequence like movies. Then he had to make an effort to remember them. Whereas now he just forgot them, and that was that.

His sleep of late had become like diving into a pitch-black mass, deprived of his senses and brain. For all practical purposes, he became a corpse.

So what did this mean?

That each time he woke up he should consider it a resurrection?

A resurrection which, in his own case, featured not the sounding of the trumpets but, 99 per cent of the time, the voice of Catarella?

But are we sure that trumpets have anything to do with the Resurrection?

Or are they only supposed to accompany the Last Judgement?

There: was it, at that very moment, the trumpets sounding or the telephone ringing?

He looked at the clock, undecided whether to go and answer the phone or not. It was seven a.m.

He went to pick it up.

But at the very moment his right hand was about to land on the receiver, his left hand, of its own initiative, reached down for the plug and pulled it out of the wall.

Montalbano stood there a moment, speechless, just look-ing at it. Sure, he didn't feel like hearing Catarella's voice reporting the daily murder, but was that any way for a hand to behave? How do you explain such an act of indepen-dence? Could it be that as old age approached, his limbs were gaining a certain autonomy?

If so, even walking would soon become a problem, with one foot wanting to go in one direction and the other in another.

He opened the French windows, went out onto the veranda, and noticed that the usual morning fisherman, Mr Puccio, had already returned and had just finished pulling his boat ashore.

The inspector went down to the beach just as he was, in his underpants.

'How'd it go?'

'My dear Inspector, the fish have all taken to the open seas by now. The water just offshore is too polluted with all our crap. So I didn't catch much.'

He thrust a hand into his boat and pulled out an octo-pus over two feet long.

'Here, this is for you.'

It was a big octopus, enough for four people.

'No thanks. What am I supposed to do with that?'

'What are you supposed to do with it? Eat it, that's what, and think of me. All you got to do is boil it for a long time. But first you got to tell your housekeeper to beat it with a cane to soften it up.'

'Listen, I really appreciate it, but——'

'Just take it,' Mr Puccio insisted.

Montalbano took it and headed back towards the veranda.

Halfway there, he felt a sharp, stabbing pain in his left foot. The octopus, which he was having trouble grasping, slipped out of his hands and fell onto the sand. Cursing the saints, Montalbano raised his leg and looked at his foot.

He had a cut on the sole, and it was bleeding. He'd stepped on the top of a rusty tin of tomatoes that some stinking son of a whore had left on the ground.

Of course the fish stayed away! By now the beaches had become the branch offices of the waste-disposal companies, and the coasts were all sewage outlets.

He bent down, picked up the octopus, and started running, with a pronounced limp, towards the house. He'd had his tetanus booster, but still it was best to be safe.

He headed to the kitchen and dumped the octopus into the sink, turning on the water to rinse it of all the sand that had stuck to its skin when he dropped it. Then he threw open the shutters, went into the bathroom, and disinfected the cut for a long time with alcohol, swearing in pain. Then he put a large plaster over it.

Now he urgently needed a coffee.

As he was preparing the espresso pot in the kitchen, he started feeling a strange apprehension that he couldn't explain.

He slowed down his movements to try and work out what was bothering him.

And he suddenly became aware of something: that two eyes were fixed firmly on him.

There was someone staring at him from outside the kitchen window. Someone standing there silently, without speaking, who therefore surely didn't have the best of intentions.

What to do?

The first thing was not to let them know that he'd noticed. Whistling the *Merry Widow* waltz, he went and lit the gas ring and put the coffeepot on the flame. He could still feel the strange eyes on the back of his neck like shotgun barrels.

He was too experienced not to realize that a hard stare like that, so still and menacing, could only come from a profound hatred. It was the stare of someone who wanted him dead.

He felt the skin under his moustache moisten with sweat.

Slowly his right hand reached for a large kitchen knife and gripped the handle tight.

If the man outside the window had a gun, he would shoot the moment Montalbano turned around.

But he had no choice.

He turned around abruptly and at the same time threw himself flat on the floor. It hurt, and the thud of his fall made the pane on the sideboard and the glasses inside tinkle.

But no shot was fired because there was nobody outside the window.

This, however, meant nothing, the inspector reasoned, because it was also possible that the man had very quick reflexes and had stepped out of his range of vision as soon as he'd seen Montalbano turn around. Now he was absolutely certain that the guy was crouching under the window, waiting for him to make the first move.

He noticed that his body, now sweating all over, was sticking to the floor.

He started to get up slowly, eyes fixed on the square of sky between the shutters, ready to spring against his enemy and fly straight out of the window, the way cops in American movies do.

At last he was on his feet when a sudden noise behind him made him start like a skittish horse. Then he realized it was just the coffee bubbling up.

He took a quick step forward and to the right.

And in this way the far edge of the sink came into his field of vision.

His blood ran suddenly cold.

Clutching the slab of marble beside the sink with its tentacles was the octopus, perfectly still, eyes fixed menacingly on him.

But there was no battle.

Montalbano cried out in terror, jumped backwards,

and crashed against the stove, upsetting the espresso pot, which spilled four or five burning drops of coffee onto his back and sent him running out of the kitchen, still screaming like a madman, and through the hallway in the grips of an uncontrollable terror to the front door, which he opened to race out of the house, when he crashed into Adelina, who was on her way in. They both fell to the ground yelling, Adelina more frightened than he was, to see him so frightened.

'Wha'ss happenin', Isspector? Wha'ss goin' on?'

He was unable to answer. He couldn't say a word.

Still lying on the ground, he was in the clutches of a laughing fit that brought tears to his eyes.

His housekeeper wasted no time grabbing the octopus and killing it with a few mallet blows to the head.

Montalbano had a shower and then subjected himself to Adelina's medical ministrations to the burn marks on his back. Then he drank a cup of coffee from a newly brewed pot and got ready to go out.

'Wha' should I do, plugga tiliphone becka in?' Adelina asked him.

'Yes.'

The telephone rang at once. He went to pick it up. It was Livia.

'Why didn't you answer earlier?' was her opening salvo.

'Earlier when?'

'Earlier.'

Matre santa, the patience you had to have with that woman!

'Could you please tell me at what time you called?'

'Around seven.'

He was worried. Why had she called so early? Had something happened? 'Why?'

'Why what?'

Shit, what a dialogue!

'Why did you call me so early?'

'Because this morning, the moment I opened my eyes, you were the first thing that came into my mind.'

For reasons unknown, Montalbano's quibbling reflex kicked into action, which risked creating unpleasant consequences.

'In other words,' he replied coldly, 'there are days when I am not the first thing that comes into your mind.'

'Oh, come on!'

'No, no, I think this is interesting. What is in fact the first thing that comes into your mind when you wake up?'

'Excuse me, Salvo, but what if I asked you the same thing?' But Livia was in no mood to quarrel and continued: 'Don't be silly. Have a good one.'

Montalbano plunged at once into a state of anguish. He'd always been hopeless with dates, holidays, birthdays, name days, anniversaries, and similar drudgeries, and always forgot them. There was nothing doing. Dense fog.

Then, suddenly, a light went on in his head: it must

be the umpteenth anniversary of their time together. How long had they been together?

Soon they could celebrate their silver anniversary of being together, if such a thing even existed.

'You too,' he said.

'What do you mean, me too?'

From Livia's answer he knew he'd made a mistake. What a tremendous pain in the arse!

It must therefore be something that concerned him poissonally in poisson. But what?

Better just bow out gracefully, with a generic thank-you.

'Thanks,' he said.

Livia started laughing.

'Oh, no you don't, my friend! You only said "thanks" to end the discussion! Whereas I bet you don't even remember what day it is today!'

It was true. He didn't.

Luckily the previous day's newspaper was on the table. Craning his neck, he managed to read the date: 5 September.

'Livia, I think you're going a little overboard! Today is the sixth . . .'

A blinding flash.

'My birthday!' he exclaimed.

'See what it took to get you to remember that today is your fifty-eighth birthday? Were you trying to repress it?'

'What do you mean, my fifty-eighth?'

'Salvo, I'm sorry, but weren't you born in 1950?'

'That's exactly right. Today I finish my fifty-seventh year on earth and enter the fifty-eighth, which I have yet to use up. I've still got twelve months ahead of me, minus a few hours, to be exact.'

'You have a strange way of counting.'

'Look, Livia, it was you who taught me to count that way!'

'It was?!'

'Oh, yes, it was your fortieth birthday, and I—'

'You're such a boor,' said Livia.

And she hung up.

Good God! Another two years and he would be sixty!

From that moment on, he was going to stop taking public transport, for fear that some young person might give him his seat upon seeing him.

Then it occurred to him that he could keep taking public transport without any worry, since the custom of giving up one's seat to the elderly had fallen out of use.

Nowadays there was no more respect for the elderly. They were roundly scorned and insulted, as if those who scorned and insulted them weren't themselves going to grow old one day.

But why was he thinking such things, anyway? Maybe because he felt that he now belonged to the category of the elderly?

His mood darkened.

*

After he'd been cruising a while on the provincial road at his usual speed, a car behind him started honking its horn to pass.

At that point the road surface narrowed because there was work in progress. In any case, he was going fifty kilometres an hour, which was the speed limit, since they were still within the Vigàta city boundary.

Therefore he didn't move an inch.

The car behind him started honking wildly; then, with a sort of roar, it pulled up beside him, practically sideswiping his car. What was this idiot trying to do, run him off the road?

The driver, who looked about thirty, leaned towards Montalbano's side and yelled:

'Get yourself to a nursing home, granddad!'

And, not satisfied with this, he grabbed a big monkey wrench and brandished it at the inspector, saying:

'I'm going to beat your brains out with this, you walking corpse!'

Montalbano couldn't react in any way; he was too busy trying to keep his car on the road.

A second later the young man's car, a powerful BMW, leapt forward and vanished in an instant, recklessly passing the entire queue ahead of him.

Montalbano wished him a happy flight into the nearest ravine. And for good measure, he wished him a nice little fire when his car hit the bottom.

But what had happened to people in this country? In

the last few years they seemed to have regressed centuries. Maybe if you took their clothes off, underneath you would find the sheepskins that primitive man used to wear.

Why so much mutual intolerance? Why was it that nobody could any longer stand his neighbour, his co-worker, or even his schoolmate?

*

Past the last houses at the edge of town, there was a rather large petrol station. The inspector noticed the BMW stopped there, filling up. He decided to keep on going; he didn't need refuelling yet. But then he changed his mind. Resentment got the better of him, and the desire to make the guy pay for his actions.

He accelerated, pulled into the station, and came to a halt with the nose of his car almost resting on that of the BMW. The young man paid and then started his car. But he couldn't move, because Montalbano's car was blocking him. Nor could he reverse, because in the meantime another car had come in behind him and was awaiting its turn at the pump.

The young man honked his horn and gestured to Montalbano to move.

The inspector pretended that his car wouldn't start.

'Tell him I have to get out!' the young man yelled to the station attendant.

But the attendant had recognized the inspector, who among other things was a regular customer, and so he pretended he hadn't heard, took the pump, and went to serve the other motorist.

Wild with rage and foaming at the mouth, the young man got out and came towards Montalbano with the monkey wrench in his hand. He raised it in the air and then brought it down with all his might.

'I told you I was going to get you!'

But instead of Montalbano's brains, what he broke was the glass on the driver's side of his car. The young guy raised his arm again and then froze.

Inside the car, the inspector was sitting in the driver's seat, calmly pointing his gun at him.

✳

Officer Gallo, having been summoned by the station attendant, arrived some ten minutes later. He handcuffed the young man and made him sit in the patrol car.

'Put him in a holding cell. And make him do a breathalyser and the other tests,' said the inspector.

Gallo was off like a rocket. He enjoyed driving fast.

✳

When Montalbano got to headquarters, Catarella, as always happened on that day of the year, rushed up to him with his hand outstretched and in an emotional state.

'My virry best wishes wit' all my 'eart for a rilly rilly long life an' alla 'appiness an' 'ealtiness inna world, Chief!'

Montalbano first shook his hand and then, out of a

sudden impulse, hugged him to his chest. Catarella started crying.

Three minutes later he was sitting in his office when Fazio came in.

'My very best wishes to you, Chief, and on behalf of the whole department,' he said.

'Thanks. Have a seat.'

'I can't, Chief. I have to go join Inspector Augello, who also told me to give you his best wishes. He's in Piano Lanterna.'

'What's he doing there?'

'A supermarket was burgled there last night.'

'What'd they steal, a few boxes of detergent?'

'No, Chief. They stole the day's revenues, a pretty good amount.'

'But aren't each day's proceeds taken to the bank in the evening?'

'Yes, but not yesterday.'

'OK, go, I'll see you later.'

'If you don't have anything better to do, I'll bring you some papers to sign.'

No, no signing! Not on his birthday!

'Let's do it another day.'

'But, Chief, some of those papers go back a whole month!'

'Has anyone made any noise about it?'

'No.'

'So what's the hurry? One day more, one day less isn't going to make any difference.'

'Chief, if the Minister for Bureaucratic Reform ever finds out, there'll be hell to pay.'

'All the minister wants to do is to speed up the uselessness, the pointless merry-go-round of documents ninety per cent of which have no purpose whatsoever.'

'Yes, but a functionary is not supposed to decide which documents are necessary and which aren't. He's just supposed to sign them.'

'And what's this functionary anyway, a robot? Doesn't he also have a brain? Doesn't he think? And when the functionary knows that those documents serve no purpose, why should he deal with them at all?'

'So what should be done, in your opinion?'

'Uselessness should be abolished.'

'Come on, Chief, that's not possible.'

'Why not?'

'Because uselessness is an integral part of man.'

Montalbano looked at him in astonishment. He was discovering Fazio the philosopher.

Fazio continued:

'Just take my advice, Chief. Don't you think it's better if you get rid of those documents little by little? I'll bring you just twenty, to get started. Half an hour is all it'll take, and you'll have them out of your hair.'

'All right, but let's make it ten.'

TWO

He'd just finished signing the papers when the telephone rang.

'Chief, 'ere's a lawyer by the name of Ne'er-Do-Well wantsa talk t'yiz poissonally in poisson.'

'Put him on.'

'I can't insomuch as it so 'appens the beforemintioned lawyer's awreddy onna primisses, Chief.'

'All right, then, send him in. Oh, but wait a second. Are you sure his name is Ne'er-Do-Well?'

"Ass rilly 'is name, Chief: Ne'er-Do-Well. Jess like I said. Y'can bet the 'ouse on it, Chief.'

'No, you can bet your own house if you like.'

The man who came in must have been about the same age as him, but was tall, slender, well dressed, and discreet in manner. The only thing that clashed with the whole was that he must have poured a good half-litre of a sickly sweet cologne over himself, which made the inspector feel like throwing up.

'May I come in? My name is Nero Duello, I'm a lawyer.' They shook hands. Good thing the lawyer hadn't given him time to open his mouth, or he would have called him Ne'er-Do-Well and the whole thing would surely have taken a bad turn.

'Please sit down, and excuse me for just a moment.'

He got up and opened the window. Otherwise he would have had to hold his breath the whole time. He inhaled a mouthful of air poisoned with car exhaust, but it was still better than that cologne. He went and sat back down.

'What can I do for you?'

'I'm here on my client's behalf.'

Montalbano paused.

'And who's your client?'

'Giovanni Strangio.'

'And who's he?'

'What do you mean, "Who's he?" You arrested him yourself barely an hour ago!'

Now it was all clear. The lawyer's client was the furious young man. But who informed the lawyer?

'I'm sorry, but how did you find out that—'

'Strangio called me himself.'

'From where?'

'From here! From the holding cell! With his mobile.'

Apparently Gallo hadn't thought to take his phone away. He made a mental note to give him a tongue-lashing.

'Listen, sir, I still haven't questioned your client yet.'

He picked up the phone.

'Catarella, send Gallo to me, would you?' As soon as the officer arrived, the inspector asked him:

'Did you have him do the breathifier?'

'You mean the breathalyser?'

'Whatever.'

For a second he felt like he was turning into Catarella. 'Came out negative, Chief.'

'And the other tests?'

'A blood sample was taken. It's being processed in Montelusa.'

'License, insurance, inspection, all in order?'

'Yes, sir, all in order.'

'All right, you can go. Ah, wait a second. Did you take his mobile from him?'

Gallo slapped himself on the forehead.

'Oh, damn!'

'Go and get it. We'll talk about this later, just the two of us.'

Gallo went out.

'You'll see that toxicology test will also come out negative,' said the lawyer.

'What makes you say that?'

'I know my client. He doesn't use drugs and never has.'

'So he's just high on life?' the inspector asked.

The lawyer threw up his hands.

'The fact, you see, is that these sorts of exploits are not new to my client.'

'You mean he often works with a monkey wrench?'

The lawyer threw up his hands again.

'He's not all there in the head.'

It was hopeless. Despite the open window, the scent of cologne had started to permeate the room. It made Montalbano feel agitated. Maybe that was what led him to say something a little over the top.

'But do you realize that this Strangio is a potential murderer? A future hit-and-run driver who won't stop to help someone he's run over?'

'Inspector, I think the language you're using is a little strong.'

'But it was you yourself, just now, who said he's not all there!'

'But that's a long way from calling him a murderer! Let me tell you something quite frankly, Inspector. I don't like one bit having someone like Giovanni Strangio as a client.'

'So why do you do it?'

'Because I'm his father's lawyer, and he begged me to—'

'And who's his father?'

'His father is Michele Strangio, president of the province.'

A few things suddenly became clear to Montalbano.

The first was the reason why, even though he was off in the head, nobody had, at the very least, taken his driver's licence away.

'So I'm here,' the lawyer resumed, 'to ask you to bury the hatchet in this whole affair.'

'If I bury any hatchet it'll be in your client's brain. Get my drift?'

But what the hell was he saying? Was it possible that particular brand of cologne somehow lowered his inhibitions?

'Please just forget the whole thing,' Nero Duello insisted, 'and we, for our part, will forget about the provocation.'

'What provocation?'

'Yours. At the petrol station. It was you, by parking your car in front of his, who prevented him from leaving. Which made my client lose his temper and . . .'

This was true. What a brilliant idea it had been for him to decide to stir things up with the young hothead! His only choice now was to start piling on a great quantity of fabrications in self-defence. But first he had to take a deep breath and calm down. He got up, went to the window, poisoned his lungs a little more, and sat back down.

'Is that all he told you?'

'Why, is there more?'

'Hell yes, there's more! And in any case there was no provocation on my part. At that moment I'd realized I had no more petrol in the tank and I botched the manoeuvre when I pulled into the station. I wanted to pull out again, but the engine wouldn't start. I have a very old car. That said, didn't your client tell you that five minutes earlier he'd tried to run me off the road?'

The lawyer grinned.

'For what happened at the pump, there's a witness. The station attendant.'

'But all the attendant witnessed was that my car wouldn't move! He certainly can't say I did it on purpose! And I'll have you know that there are two witnesses to the fact that your client tried to run me off the road!'

'Really?'

The lawyer's question had a note of irony. So Montalbano decided to try a desperate bluff. Looking Nero Duello straight in the eye, he opened the top drawer of his desk, pulled out two sheets of paper at random, and starting reading one:

'I, the undersigned, Antonio Passaloca, son of Carmelo Passaloca and Agata née Conigliaro, born in Vigàta on 12 September 1950 and residing there at Via Martiri di Belfiore 18, declare the following: at around nine o'clock this morning, as I was driving on the provincial road towards Vigàta—'

'That's quite enough,' said the lawyer.

He'd swallowed it, had the good lawyer. Montalbano put the paper back into the drawer. He'd pulled it off!

Nero Duello heaved a sigh and took a different tack.

'All right then. I take back what I said about provocation.'

He leaned his upper body towards the inspector and

rested his arms on the desk. He bent forward, and that movement unleashed a blast of cologne straight into Montalbano's nostrils and down into the pit of his stomach, stirring up a wave of nausea that rose into his throat.

'But I'm begging you, Inspector, to try and understand. Because if people like us, who've already reached a certain age, can't be understanding, who—'

He'd said the very words he shouldn't have. Between the allusion to old age and the retching reflex, Montalbano couldn't hold back any longer.

'Me, be understanding? Me, a certain age? You know what? I'm going to ask for the maximum sentence for your client! The maximum!'

The lawyer stood up, worried.

'Are you feeling all right, Inspector?'

'I feel great! You'll see how great I feel!'

He opened the door and yelled into the hall.

'Gallo!'

The officer came running.

'Get the detainee and take him to Montelusa prison. At once!'

Then, turning to the lawyer.

'I think your business is finished here.'

'Good day,' Nero Duello said drily, going out.

Montalbano left the door open to air the room out a little.

Then he sat down and started writing the report. He

slipped in a good ten possible crimes. He signed it and sent it to the prosecutor's office.

That should fix Giovanni Strangio.

✳

Around noon a call came in.

'Chief, 'at'd be a soitan Mr Porcellino 'oo wantsa talk t'yiz poissonally in poisson.'

Montalbano didn't trust him.

'Cat, is this a repeat performance?'

'When wazza foist one, Chief?'

'The first one was when you called the lawyer Ne'er-Do-Well instead of Nero Duello.'

'But 'ass azackly what I said! Ne'er-Do-Well!'

How could you reason with a person like that?

'Are you sure this man's name really is Porcellino?'

'Assolutely, Chief. I swear on my mama's head.'

'Did he tell you what he wanted?'

'Nah, 'e din't say, but 'e sounded like 'e was rilly teed off. Like a lion inna jangle, Chief.'

The inspector really didn't feel like taking the call, but then his sense of duty won out.

'Montalbano here. What can I do for you, Mr Porcellino?'

'Porcellino?! So now you're going to start fucking me about as well?' the man said furiously. 'Borsellino's the name! Guido Borsellino!'

OK, that would teach him never, not even for a second, to trust Catarella, who always mangled people's names.

'I'm terribly sorry, sir, really, but our receptionist must have heard wrong. What can I do for you?'

'I'm being accused of the most incredible things! They're treating me like a thief! I demand that you, who are their superior, apologize at once!'

Apologize? The inspector's balls immediately took off into a spin, a sort of rocket blast-off.

'Listen, Mr Por — er, Borsellino, I suggest you wash your face, calm down, and then call back.'

'I'm not—'

Montalbano hung up.

*

Not five minutes later, the phone rang again. This time it was Fazio.

'Sorry, Chief, but . . .'

Apparently it wasn't an easy call to make for Fazio. 'What is it?'

'Could you come here to the supermarket?'

'Why?'

'The manager's making a stink because Inspector Augello asked him a couple of questions he didn't appreciate. He says he won't talk unless his lawyer is present.'

'Listen, is this manager's name Borsellino?'

'Yes, sir.'

'He called just now to break my balls.'

'What do you say, Chief, will you come?'

'I'll be there in ten minutes.'

*

As he was heading towards Piano Lanterna, he remembered that people about town had been whispering that that supermarket was owned by a company made up entirely of front men, since the people who had actually put up the money for it all belonged to the Cuffaro family, which divided up all the business in town with its enemies, the Sinagra family. He was driving through the part of Piano Lanterna where four horrendous dwarf high-rises — or rather, abortions of high-rises — had been built to house the population that had almost entirely deserted the centre of town to move to the upland plain.

Once upon a time, to judge from photos and from what the headmaster Burgio, an elderly friend of his, had told him, the whole elevated part consisted of only two rows of small houses flanking the road to the cemetery. And all around were large open spaces for bocce and football games, family outings, duels, and epic clashes between feuding families.

Now it was a sea of cement, a sort of casbah dominated by fake high-rises.

*

The supermarket was closed, but the policeman on duty took him to the manager's office.

Passing through the shop, he saw Fazio questioning some cashiers.

In the manager's office he found Mimì Augello sitting in a chair in front of a desk, behind which sat a very thin man of about fifty without a hair on his head, wearing very thick-lensed glasses. He was quite upset.

As soon as he saw the inspector walk in he shot to his feet.

'I want my lawyer!'

'Have you accused Mr Borsellino of something?' the inspector asked his deputy.

'I haven't accused him of anything,' replied Mimì, cool as a cucumber. 'I merely asked him two or three simple questions, and he—'

'Simple questions, you call them!' cried Borsellino.

' – he got upset. Anyway, it was him who called us to report the burglary.'

'And so if somebody calls you to report a burglary, you feel obliged to accuse the victim of perpetrating the crime?'

'I did nothing of the sort,' replied Mimì. 'You arrived at that conclusion all by yourself.'

'What else could I conclude?'

'Excuse me just a minute,' said Montalbano. 'Let me get this straight. Mr Borsellino, I want you to repeat to me what you said to Inspector Augello. How did you discover you'd been robbed?'

Borsellino first took a deep breath to calm his nerves, then spoke.

'Since there were quite a few items on sale yesterday, by the end of the day my receipts were considerable.'

'How much?'

Borsellino looked at a sheet of paper on the desk.

'Sixteenthousandsevenhundredandtwentyeight euros and thirty cents.'

'All right. And what do you normally do with the day's proceeds? Do you go and deposit them every evening in your bank's night safe?'

'Of course.'

'And why not yesterday?'

'*Madonna biniditta!* I explained that to this gentleman here! How many times do I have to say it?'

'Mr Borsellino, I already told you on the phone to calm down. It's in your own interest.'

'What do you mean by that?'

'Emotion gives bad advice. In your agitation you might say something you don't want to say.'

'That's why I want my lawyer!'

'Mr Borsellino, nobody is accusing you of anything, so you don't need any lawyer. Don't be silly! You know something?'

But he didn't tell him straight off. He started staring at the stamp on an envelope that lay on the desk.

'Do I know what?' asked the manager.

Montalbano took his eyes off the envelope and looked at him.

'To me you don't seem so upset about the burglary. You seem scared.'

'Me?! Scared of what?'

'I don't know, it's just my impression. Shall we go on? Or should we go down to headquarters and continue there?'

'Let's go on.'

'I asked you why you didn't deposit the money.'

'Ah, yes. When I got to the night safe, there was a sign that said out of order. What choice did I have? I came back here, put the money into this drawer of the desk, locked it, and went home. This morning, about an hour after I came in – or maybe longer, I don't remember – I realized that someone had forced open the drawer and stolen the money. And I called your police station, with the fine results we see here!'

Montalbano turned to Augello.

'Did you phone the bank?'

'Of course! And they told me the night safe worked just fine last night – they knew nothing about any sign saying out of order.'

'I swear on my mother's blessed soul that there was a sign!' said Borsellino.

'I'm not doubting you,' said Montalbano.

The man was stumped.

'You believe me?'

Montalbano didn't answer, but went and looked at the lock that had been forced. Whoever did it must not have had much trouble opening it; a hairpin would have done the trick.

Inside the drawer, on top of a few invoices, was thirty euro cents in change.

'So what did you ask Mr Borsellino to get him so upset?' Montalbano asked Augello.

'I simply asked him, given that nobody other than himself knew that the money was in that drawer, and given that there are no signs of any of the outside doors of the supermarket having been forced – I simply asked him whether he could explain to me how and in what fashion the burglars, in his opinion, could have got inside, and how they knew that the money hadn't been deposited but was here instead.'

'That's all?'

'That's all, not one word more, or less.'

'And you got all worked up over a perfectly normal question?' Montalbano asked Borsellino.

'I got worked up not only over the words but the look!' the manager reacted.

'The look?'

'Yes, sir, the look! As he was asking the question, he was looking at me as if to say: I know it was you who did it, so don't think you can fool me.'

'The furthest thing from my mind,' said Augello. 'He imagined that look himself.'

The inspector assumed an episcopal air, exactly like the Good Shepherd.

'Look, Mr Borsellino, you're too upset, which is perfectly understandable after being shaken up by a burglary, but you mustn't let yourself get so carried away. You're all worked up and take every word, every gesture, even the most innocent, the wrong way. Try to calm down and answer my question: who has the keys to the supermarket?'

'I do.'

'Aren't there any copies?'

'Yes, one set. The company's board of directors has them.'

'I see. So how do you explain it?'

'Explain what?'

'That the doors show no sign of having been forced.'

'No idea.'

'Let me ask you the same question in a different way. Is it possible the thieves used copies of the keys?'

Before answering, the manager thought this over for a minute.

'Well, yes.'

'The ones belonging to the board of directors?'

THREE

Upon hearing the question, Borsellino literally leapt out of his chair. He'd turned pale as a corpse. His hands started trembling.

Noticing, he thrust them in his pockets.

'Who told you that?'

'What do you mean who told me that? You did!'

'No, sir, I did not! I said nothing of the sort. Mr Augello is my witness!'

'Keep me out of this,' said Mimì. 'Because I'm in total agreement with the inspector: you said it yourself just a minute ago.'

'You two want me dead!' yelled Borsellino, who was sweating as if in the August sun. 'All I said was that maybe they came in with copies of the keys, but I certainly wasn't referring to the board of directors' copies! I meant some other copies!'

'Then you made a false declaration when you said that

there was only one set of copies, when in fact there are at least two!' said Montalbano.

Borsellino took his hands out of his pockets and put his palms against his forehead as if he had a terrible headache. 'No, no, no! You two are trying to make me lose my mind! You want to see me sentenced to death! I said, and I repeat, that the burglars could have used copies they made themselves for that purpose!'

'Forgive me for insisting,' said Montalbano. 'But in order to make copies, you need originals. Doesn't that make sense? So there's no getting around it: either you gave the burglar the original keys or somebody from the board of directors did. What do you think?'

'I want my lawyer!'

Montalbano huffed in annoyance.

'Well, Mimì, I guess we can go. There's nothing left for us to do here.'

Augello got up without a word.

Borsellino, for his part, stood there for a moment looking at them, speechless, then began to protest.

'What is this? Why?'

'Mr Borsellino,' Montalbano said after staring at him in turn for a moment, 'I sincerely don't understand you. First you want a lawyer and then you complain that we're too hasty? I can well understand that you feel reassured by our presence, but I'm sorry, we can't stay any longer. Let's go, Mimì.'

But Borsellino had no intention of giving up.

'Excuse me, but would you please explain why I should feel reassured by your presence?'

Montalbano rolled his eyes up to heaven.

'Mr Borsellino, with you one needs more patience than even the saints possess! You've just finished accusing us of wanting you sentenced to death. And you are very clearly scared out of your wits. All I did was do the maths. Which tells me that as long as we remain here, nobody can do anything to you. Get the picture?'

'And what would anyone want to do to me?'

Borsellino was going from fear to defiance.

'Whatever the case,' the inspector continued, 'was a report drafted of your complaint?'

'Yes, but—'

'Have you informed your company chairman that a theft took place?'

'Not yet.'

Montalbano showed great surprise.

'Ah ah ah! You never cease to amaze me!'

'Why?'

'Because it's the first thing you should have done! Even before calling us.'

'I'll do it as soon as—'

'It may be too late, you know. There's no point in putting off the moment of truth.'

The shop manager started turning visibly pale again.

'But the first thing I did was call you!'

'But we're not them, don't you see?'

Borsellino turned even paler and his hands started shaking more violently.

'Th . . . them? Who's them?'

'Them,' the inspector said evasively. 'You know perfectly well who they are. And they'll ask you questions that'll make ours seem like a walk in the park by comparison.'

Borsellino took a handkerchief out of his pocket and wiped the sweat glistening on his brow. His nose was starting to drip.

Montalbano threw down his ace.

'And those guys, you can bet your life they won't let you call your lawyer.'

He let out a laugh, sounding like a starving hyena in the desert, and continued:

'At best they'll call you a priest for the last rites. I don't envy you. Have a good day.'

And he started heading for the door.

'Wa . . . wait,' Borsellino gasped, collapsing into a chair. 'I swear on my mother's blessed soul that I wasn't the one who stole the—'

'But I'm well aware of that!' the inspector exclaimed. 'In fact I'm totally convinced of it! You're not so stupid as to go and steal money from the Cuffaros. You did make things easy for the burglar, however. And he mustn't be just any burglar – burglars know that you don't just go and rob the Cuffaros. It must be someone who can easily get his hands on the other keys, of which the board of directors owns the second set, take them for about an hour, use them, and then put them back without anyone noticing. Someone in the family, in other words, who urgently needed some of the company's money and therefore took it. A traitor. Who will meet the same end as other traitors to the family.'

Head hanging against his chest, Borsellino was now having trouble holding back the tears.

'Best of luck,' said Montalbano, leaving the office.

*

'My heartfelt compliments, maestro. That was a textbook interrogation,' said Augello as soon as they were outside. 'But would you explain to me why you didn't keep going? The man was completely fried.'

'First of all, because I felt sorry for him. Secondly, because he was never going to name the person who made him do what he did, not even if we tortured him.'

They were joined by Fazio.

'Did he confess?'

'No, but he was just about to.'

'I wonder how they forced him,' said Augello.

'Probably blackmail. Fazio, see if you can find out more about this Borsellino.'

'Still,' said Mimì, 'there's something in all this that doesn't make sense to me.'

'And what's that?'

'Why bother to use duplicate keys? They'd already

gone so far as to put the fake sign on the night-deposit box and force open the drawer, they might as well have gone all the way and broken the outside locks. Whereas they did it the way they did so that we would immediately think of the extra set of keys in the hands of the board of directors and the complicity of the manager. But it was a huge mistake!'

Montalbano glared at him.

'You think it was a mistake?'

Augello bristled.

'Do you have a better idea?'

'Well, half an idea, to be exact.'

'And what would that be?'

'That the fact there was no break-in caught the manager by surprise, too. He hadn't expected that. The agreement made with the burglar must certainly have stipulated that one of the supermarket's outside locks would be broken. That's why he was so scared.'

'But what does it mean?'

'I don't know yet. Listen, I'm going to get something to eat. I'll see you two later this afternoon.'

*

'Why so late?' asked Enzo, the restaurateur, upon seeing the inspector come in.

Montalbano felt his heart give a tug.

'Why, is there nothing left? Did your customers eat everything?'

'Not to worry, Inspector. For you there's always something to eat.'

Seafood antipasto (double portion), pasta with sea urchin sauce (a portion and a half), and red mullet cooked in salt (six rather large fish).

He asked for the bill. He'd allowed himself a special birthday feast. And, indeed, as he was getting up from the table, he saw Enzo approaching with a tiny little cake, enough for one.

'With my very best wishes, Inspector.'

He realized he couldn't very well shun Enzo's offering. He had to eat that cake, even if it risked ruining the wonderful taste of mullet in his mouth.

His mood, moreover, had already been ruined by the two candles on the cake, one shaped like a 5, the other like an 8, forming the number 58.

Apparently Enzo counted the same way as Livia.

The walk along the jetty thus became necessary not only for digestive reasons but also to shake off the irritation that the number on the cake had caused him.

*

As soon as he sat back down at his desk, Gallo came in.

'Chief, I have something to tell you about Giovanni Strangio.'

'Tell me.'

'You ordered me to take him to Montelusa prison, but

as soon as I got there and introduced myself, they told me I had to take him to the prosecutor's office.'

'Which prosecutor?'

'Dr Seminara.'

Montalbano screwed up his face. It was well known that Prosecutor Seminara was rather sensitive to the pressures of a certain political party. Apparently Nero Duello had already informed him. 'And what did he do?'

'He immediately released him.'

'But did he read what I wrote?'

'Yes, sir. He had it on his desk.'

'So in spite of my report, he released him?'

Gallo threw up his hands.

'OK, thanks.'

Montalbano decided to set his mind at rest. All this meant was that when Strangio finally killed someone, it would be on Prosecutor Seminara's conscience.

Gallo was still on his way out when the telephone rang.

'Ahh, Chief! Ahh, Chief, Chief!'

This was the classic Catarellian litany whenever Hizzoner the C'mishner, as he called him, was on the phone.

'Tell him I'm not in the office.'

'Bu', Chief, ya gotta unnastan', 'e's rilly pissed off!'

'Well, just piss him off a little more.'

'*Matre santa*, Chief, the guy's libel a eat me right true the tiliphone line!'

*

Fazio came back in around six in the evening.

'What did you find out about Borsellino?'

Fazio sat down, stuck a hand in his pocket, and pulled out a small sheet of paper.

'I'm warning you,' said the inspector, 'if you start reading me his date and place of birth and mother's and father's names, I'm going to take that piece of paper out of your hands, crumple it up into a ball, and make you eat it.'

'Whatever you say, Chief,' said Fazio, half-resigned, half-offended.

He folded it up and put it back in his pocket.

He suffered from what the inspector called a 'records office complex'. If, for example, Montalbano wanted simply to know what someone had done at eleven the previous morning, Fazio, in his report, would start with the man's date of birth, then his parents, their address, and so on and so forth.

'And so?' the inspector coaxed him.

'Widower, fifty years old, no children, no known girl-friends or vices,' said Fazio, telegraphic in his resentment.

'And what do they say about him around town?'

'That he was hired by the supermarket at the urging of the Honourable Mongibello.'

The Honourable Mongibello, formerly of the Liberal Party, then the Christian Democratic Party, and then, after some time off, elected to Parliament in the last elections as a deputy for the majority party, the one trying to force

Italy into a straitjacket, had long been, and still was, a faithful lawyer of the Cuffaro family.

'OK, but before being hired as manager, what did he do?'

'He worked in Sicudiana as an accountant for a number of businesses belonging to the Cuffaros.'

'So, a kind of loyal servant?'

'Apparently.'

'Listen, could you try and find out who is on the board of directors of the—'

'Already taken care of.'

Now that he'd had some measure of revenge, Fazio relaxed.

'Who are they?'

'Chief, I wrote their names down on that piece of paper. Can I take it back out?'

Montalbano had no choice but to swallow Fazio's sarcasm.

'All right.'

'The board of directors are Angelo Farruggia, Filippo Tridicino, Gerlando Prosecuto, and Calogero Lauricella. The first two are eighty-year-old retired railwaymen, Prosecuto is a projectionist at the cinema, and Lauricella formerly worked as a warehouseman at the fish market. All front men.'

'And who's the president?'

'The Honourable Mongibello.'

Montalbano hesitated.

'I wonder why he decided to expose himself person-ally?'

'Maybe because on a board of directors you need at least one person who can read and write.'

*

He laid the table on the veranda, took a plate with a large serving of octopus from the fridge and brought it outside, then sat down and dressed it with olive oil and lemon juice. He started eating it with a sense of satisfaction, relishing a sort of revenge on the creature after the morning's scare. It was very tender; Adelina had cooked it perfectly.

Suddenly he remembered having read, in a book by a scientist named Alleva who worked with animals, that octopuses are extremely intelligent. He sat there a moment with his fork in midair. He reflected that it was always the fate of the intelligent to be eaten in every way possible by the more cunning cretins. He had no problem acknowledg-ing the fact that he was a cretin himself, and resumed eating.

In any case, hard as it was to digest, the octopus would have its revenge in turn, by preventing him from sleeping. A draw.

He'd just finished clearing the table and was quietly smoking a cigarette when the telephone rang. Instinctively, he looked at his watch. It was nine thirty. Too early for Livia.

'Ah, Chief! I beck yer partin' for disturbin' yiz! Wha', d'jou eat yet?'

'Yeah, Cat, don't worry about it. What is it?'

'I jess now got a call from a lady says she's a killin' lady at the supermarket in Piano Lanterna!'

'I think you mean a cleaning lady, Cat.'

'Why, wha'd I jess say?'

'Never mind. What did she want?'

'She wannit a tell us Porcellino 'ung 'isself.'

Montalbano wasn't surprised. In a way he'd expected something like that. 'Is Fazio still at the office?'

'Nossir, Chief, 'e left on 'is way to the scene wit' Gallo.'

*

When he pulled up outside the supermarket, the newsmen were already there along with fifty or so onlookers who Gallo and another police officer were keeping at bay.

Inside he found Fazio standing in front of a woman of about forty seated on a chair with her blouse unbuttoned. Beside her, another woman was holding a wet cloth to her forehead, while a third woman fanned her face with a newspaper.

Every so often the first woman would strike herself in the chest and say:

'My God, what a fright! Nearly scared me to death!'

'Was she the one who discovered the body?' the inspector asked Fazio.

'Yes, sir. But it was that girl over there who called us.'

And he gestured towards a thirtyish young woman leaning against a counter with a broom in her hand.

'Have you informed the prosecutor and Dr Pasquano?'

'Already taken care of.'

He went over to the girl.

'I'm Inspector Montalbano.'

'My name is Graziella Cusumano.'

'Please tell me how you discovered . . .'

'Me an' th'other girls come in every night aroun' nine. We knock at the back door an' the manager comes an' opens up for us. But tonight we knocked and knocked an' nobody came.'

'Had that ever happened before?'

'Nossir, never.'

'Go on.'

'So we thought that the manager maybe went home, 'cause 'e didn't feel so good after the robbery an' all, an' I—'

'Who told you about the robbery?'

'Everybody in town knows about it, Inspector! So, anyway, I called him on my mobile, but there was no answer. An' that seemed strange to me. To be on the safe side, I decided to call the company an' explained everything to Filippo Tridicino, who's a distant relative of mine. He came wit' the key an' opened up. Filumena went to clean the manager's office, since that's her job, and when she saw him hangin' there, she fainted. An' that's when I called you.'

'What time does the supermarket close?'

'At eight. But it wasn't open this afternoon.'

'Why not?'

'I dunno. My cousin, who works at the shop as a cashier, told me. The manager told all the staff that we wouldn't be opening again after lunch.'

'Thanks,' said Montalbano, and he headed for the manager's office.

*

Borsellino had climbed onto a chair that he'd put on the desk, threaded a rope around a beam, looped the other end around his neck, kicked the chair away, and that was that.

Montalbano sat down, lit a cigarette, and started studying the corpse – which was swaying ever so slightly first to the right, then to the left, pushed back and forth by a gentle draft.

Fazio came in.

'I took statements from all the women. Shall I let them go?'

'OK.'

Fifteen minutes later, Dr Pasquano arrived, fit to be tied.

'There I am, on my way to the club for an important game, only to have you get on my case!'

'Me, on your case? If anything, it's this corpse here that has.'

Pasquano had a look at the body.

'Well, looks like a suicide, no?'

44

'Doctor, you'll have to forgive me, but it's very important to me to know at what time of day he died,' said Montalbano.

'Why?'

'Because that's how I feel. I want to be certain about the time of death.'

'I see. But if the prosecutor doesn't get here, I—'

'Doctor, don't you think you could get a closer look if you climbed up onto the desk?'

Swearing, the doctor climbed onto the desk with Fazio's help and started slowly turning the body like a large, hanging salami.

'What time is it?' he asked.

'Quarter to eleven.'

'In my opinion – but I can't really be sure of it until after the post-mortem – he hanged himself between four and five o'clock this afternoon.'

'He couldn't have done it around one?'

'I would rule that out.'

'Thanks. Fazio, I'm going home. You wait here for Prosecutor Tommaseo. Good night, Doctor.'

'Hey, what the hell! Would somebody please help me down from here?' asked the enraged Pasquano.

FOUR

He got home too early to go to bed. It would have been a mistake, anyway: he could still feel the octopus struggling in his stomach.

He got undressed and had a wash, and then, since it was midnight, he turned on the television.

Immediately the chicken-arse face of Pippo Ragonese, the purse-lipped prince of opinion of TeleVigàta News and Montalbano's sworn enemy, appeared on the screen.

. . . is the question this evening. I will review the events as objectively as possible. Upon discovering that the prior day's proceeds had been stolen during the night, the manager of the Piano Lanterna supermarket, Guido Borsellino, informed the Vigàta Police, and Inspector Augello, the second-in-command of the force, arrived on the scene. After less than half an hour of discussion with Borsellino, the inspector was practically accusing him, in veiled fashion, of having committed the burglary himself. In dismay, Borsellino called Chief Inspector Montalbano, who basically hung up on him. A short while later, however, the peerless Inspector

Montalbano turned up at the supermarket, and the two police detectives, without a shred of proof – proof, what am I saying? – without so much as a clue, began to torture – that's the exact word to use – to torture poor Mr Borsellino with such ferocity that once the interrogation was over, the poor man, upset and out of his mind from the horrible accusations, dismissed his employees for the rest of the day, went into his office, and hanged himself.

Now, even admitting, for purely academic reasons, as pure hypothesis, that Mr Borsellino, who had no record and was considered a man of great integrity by all, had given in to a momentary temptation and actually committed the theft, this would in no way justify the actions of the inspector and his deputy, which I would characterize as worthy of the Nazis.

This death is on Inspector Montalbano's conscience, and I assume full responsibility for this statement. As for his uncivilized, inhumane methods, which dishonour and besmirch our country's entire police force, an institution that has always . . .

Before turning the TV off, Montalbano spat at the newsman's face, recalling that Ragonese had applauded the police after the 'Mexican butchery' they'd imported to Genoa for the G8 summit in 2001.

But he was also convinced that the rascal's version of events had been passed to him under the table by someone else. All Ragonese had done was read it.

Clearly showing through the words of Ragonese was the very argument that would be put forward by the Cuffaros' lawyers, with Mongibello leading the pack. Borsellino himself had stolen the money, and he hadn't been able to withstand the third degree given him by Montalbano and Augello. The family couldn't admit to having been betrayed by one of their own; it would have been seen by all as a grave loss of authority.

In due time, they would quietly take care of the traitor.

For the first time in his life, a rage too long repressed played a dirty joke on the inspector. He had to run into the bathroom, where he started spitting out all the bitter bile that had come up into his mouth.

And as he knelt there on the floor with his head half inside the toilet bowl, the telephone started ringing.

He didn't manage to answer in time, and the ringing stopped. After he washed his face, it started again.

It was Livia.

'What were you doing a minute ago, when you didn't pick up?'

'Do you really want to know? I was spitting up bile.'

Livia got worried.

'Oh my God! Why?'

The question made Montalbano angry.

'Just for fun.'

'Don't be such an idiot! Are you ill?'

'Yes.'

'Did you eat too much?'

'No, but I had too much to swallow.'

'I don't understand.'

He told her the whole story, starting with the morning

encounter with Strangio, getting it all off his chest and barely managing not to cry in rage.

When the conversation was over, he went and sat on the veranda, smoking a cigarette. Why, he wondered, did Ragonese, and so many others like him of greater importance who wrote for the national newspapers and appeared on more widely watched television programmes, do their jobs the way they did? A serious journalist would have phoned him to learn his version of events, and only after hearing both sides of the story would he have expressed his opinion.

Whereas journalists like Ragonese only listened to one side of the story: their bosses' side. And often you couldn't even say they were doing it for the money.

Why, then? There was only one answer: because they had a servant's mentality. They were enthusiastic volunteers of servility; they fell to their knees in the face of Power, no matter which.

And they couldn't do anything about it: they were born that way.

Whatever the case, when the inspector went to bed half an hour later, he fell asleep almost immediately. Apparently his bout of rage had aided his digestion.

＊

As soon as he was inside the door of police headquarters, just before nine, Catarella intoned the litany:

'Ahh, Chief! Ahh, Chief, Chief!'

There was no need for the inspector to ask him who had phoned.

'When did he call?'

'Juss now!'

'What's he want?'

"E wants ya t'bestake yisself straightawayslike an' immidiotly t'is office, 'is meanin' 'im, meanin' Hizzoner the C'mishner.'

'All right, then, I'll go. I'll be back as soon as I can get free.'

As he started the car, he noticed he'd run out of petrol. All things considered, the nearest garage was the one where he'd had the run-in with Strangio. Speaking of which, he really had to have that window replaced; it was cracked, making it rather dangerous to keep driving around with it in that condition.

There was no wait; the attendant, whose name was Luicino, came up to his car at once.

'Top it up, Inspector?'

'Yes.'

When it came time to pay, Luicino shook his head, as if to say he didn't want any money. What was this?

'It's a present, Inspector, from me to you.'

Montalbano started the car, went and put it in the parking area, then dug into his wallet, took out the money – having earlier read the amount on the pump – got out of the car, and went back to the filling area.

The attendant was in his booth. Without a word, but

glaring hard at him, Montalbano plopped the notes down in front of him. Luicino looked at them and, without so much as taking a breath, put the money into a pocket of his greasy overalls.

'Now explain to me the reason for this grand gesture on your part.'

Luicino seemed very ill at ease.

'Inspector, it's 'cause yesterday I didn't act right. I wanted to say I was sorry.'

'For what?'

'For what I told the lawyer.'

'The lawyer of the kid with the BMW?'

'Yes, sir.'

'What did you tell him?'

'I told him you parked in front of his car, and that was why he couldn't pull out.'

'So? You told him the truth.'

'But I didn't even want to tell him that! I wanted to deny everything out of respect for you! I wanted to say I didn't see nothing!'

'So why did you change your mind?'

'He made me!'

'How?'

'He mentioned my complaint with the province, which wants to close this garage. 'Cause I made an appeal. And this lawyer knew all about the case, to the point that he told me that if I didn't . . .'

'I'll be seeing you, Luì,' said Montalbano.

He got back in his car and drove to Montelusa.

Nice people! They made no bones about blackmailing some poor bastard if he didn't do as they said. The lawyer Nero Duello could soak himself in all the cologne he wanted, he would still come out smelling like a sewer. Him and his boss, the honourable president of the province.

*

'The commissioner is busy at the moment. He told me to tell you not to leave, but to please have a seat in the waiting room,' said an usher sitting outside the door to the office.

The waiting room was so dingy that after Montalbano had been in it barely five minutes he started having suicidal thoughts.

On the little table was one lone magazine: *Polizia Moderna*. The inspector started reading it from page one. By the time he'd finished, an hour had gone by.

He got up and went over to the usher.

'Still busy?'

'Yes. He asked whether you were already here and wants you to keep waiting.'

'How much longer will he be?'

'If you ask me, another two hours.'

'Thanks.'

He went out into the hallway and instead of going back to the waiting room he kept walking, took the stairs to the ground floor, went outside, got in his car, and drove back to Vigàta.

*

He'd been back in his office for about half an hour when Dr Pasquano rang. This was unusual. Whenever Montalbano wanted to know the results of a post-mortem, he had to go to the doctor's lab and put up with a barrage of insults, slights, and obscenities before he got any information.

Pasquano not only did not have a nice disposition, but his customary bad mood always worsened if he had lost at poker the previous evening at the club.

'I wanted to duly inform you that yesterday evening, in spite of your untimely efforts at aggravation, I still had time to go to the club and win. Three hours of pure luck. I had a full house, four of a kind, and a royal flush!'

'Congratulations on your run of luck.'

'You can even call it by its proper name: *culo*.'

And he hung up. But Montalbano kept his hand close to the receiver, because he'd realized that that phone call was all theatre. In fact, less than a minute later, the phone rang again.

'Ah, I almost forgot. I had also wanted to tell you — quite secondarily, mind you — that this morning I worked on the body of the hanged man. I confirm it.'

'You confirm what?'

'That he got himself hanged, so to speak, around four in the afternoon. He still had what little he'd eaten for lunch in his stomach.'

'Why do you say he *got himself hanged*?'

'Does the idea upset you? Don't play innocent with me! And don't tell me you didn't suspect as much!'

'OK, I won't. But what did you discover?'

'I think he was strangled with somebody's bare hands. They immobilized him by holding his arms so tight that they left bruises. There were at least two killers. The rope, the beam, and the chair were all props to make it look like a suicide.'

'Are you one hundred per cent certain?'

'No. In fact I'm not going to mention it in the report.'

'Why not?'

'Because in court a good lawyer could come up with a hundred explanations for the bruises.'

'But if you don't express your opinion officially, how am I going to take any action?'

'Up yours,' said Dr Pasquano, with his customarily exquisite politeness.

And he hung up.

*

'I heard that complete bastard Ragonese on TV last night,' Mimì Augello said as he came in. 'Can't we do anything to defend ourselves?'

'What do you want to do? Sue him? You'd be lucky if the law gave you satisfaction in three or four years, by which time everyone will have forgotten the whole thing.'

'It makes my palms itch so badly I can't tell you. One

of these days, if I see him in the street, I'm going to knock him out.'

'Mimì, if your palms itch, get your wife to scratch them. Anyway, aside from the nonsense and insults, Ragonese gave you the answer you were looking for.'

'Gave *me* the answer?!'

'Yes indeed. Yesterday you said you had your doubts about the fact that the outside door hadn't been forced, and you said they'd made a big mistake by using the keys. Whereas Ragonese indirectly let you know that the thief purposely arranged things to set Borsellino up and make him look like the culprit.'

'That makes me feel even worse! It means that not only is that journalist an idiot, but he's a rogue with multiple ties to the Cuffaros.'

'Those are *your* conclusions,' said Montalbano.

Mimì went out even more upset than when he'd come in, practically colliding with Fazio in the doorway.

'You've come at just the right moment,' the inspector said to Fazio. 'There's something I need to know. Try and find out what night-time security service the supermarket employs.'

Fazio smiled.

'Already taken care of.'

Fazio was undoubtedly a terrifically good policeman, but whenever he used that phrase, it made Montalbano want to box his ears, just as Mimì wanted to do to Ragonese.

'So tell me.'

'There's nobody, Chief. There was no need. Everybody knew that the supermarket belonged to the Cuffaros. And so no thief in his right mind would ever dream of burgling it. However . . .'

'However?'

'Right next door there's a branch office of the Banca Regionale. And you can be sure they subscribe to a night-time security service. Any nightwatchman checking on the bank would have to pass in front of the supermarket. Shall I look into it?'

'Yes.'

At that moment the outside line rang. Montalbano picked up the receiver almost automatically. He froze in terror. What he was hearing was surely a human voice, but one that was imitating some enormous prehistoric animal along the lines of *Tyrannosaurus rex*.

'Mooooo . . . aaaaa . . . nooooo!'

Moano? Was that a surname? Or the masculine form of Moana?

Good thing he wasn't Moano, because talking to a Judgement Day trumpet would have been rather awkward.

'You have the wrong number,' he said.

And he hung up.

'Shall I go, then?' Fazio asked.

'Go.'

Fazio left and the phone rang again. When he picked

up the receiver, Montalbano held it at a safe distance from his ear, as a precaution.

'Inspector Montalbano? This is Lattes.'

The chief of Hizzoner Mr C'mishner's cabinet was nicknamed 'Lattes e Mieles' for his priestly, simpering way of talking.

'What can I do for you, sir?'

'The commissioner wants to see you at once. He asked me to call you, because he had to run to the toilet.'

He couldn't hold it in? This was no doubt precious information, but Montalbano didn't quite know what to do with it. Then he had a revelation that made his blood turn cold.

'Was . . . he . . . the p . . . person who rang me a moment ago?'

'Yes.'

Matre santa, what had happened to him? Had he turned into a giant reptile?

'I'm sorry, but why was the commissioner talking that way?'

'Because he was beside himself with anger. Because of you.'

'Me?!'

'It is my duty to inform you that the commissioner is very angry with you for the mess you've made—'

'That *I've* made?! What have I—'

'And above all because you were unwilling to wait for his meeting to end, as he had asked you to do.'

'But—'

'And why did you hang up on him just a few minutes ago? Come without a moment's delay, I beg you. Come immediately. Fly. For the love of God, don't make him even more upset!'

'But the fact is that I took him for a—'

He managed to stop himself in time. Could he really say he'd mistaken him for a dinosaur?

'Come at once, please.'

What the fuck! So that wild, tropical-forest voice belonged to Hizzoner the C'mishner Bonetti-Alderighi? You could say a great many things about the man, but not that he was uncivilized. The man must be enraged to death. Two options, therefore, remained for the inspector: either go and let himself be mauled like an ancient Roman in the Colosseum, or shoot himself immediately in the head. He opted for the first.

*

Dr Lattes was pacing back and forth in the waiting room when Montalbano came in. He seemed a bit worried.

'I gave him a couple of tranquillizers. He's a little better now, thank God.'

'But what did I do to him?'

'He'll tell you himself. You can go in, he's waiting for you.'

Bonetti-Alderighi was sitting behind his desk in his

armchair, a little bottle of pills and a glass of water on the desktop in front of him.

He was dishevelled, eyes slightly protruding, tie loosened and jerked to one side, top shirt button unbuttoned. He who was always so impeccably dressed! But aside from this, he looked normal enough. As soon as he saw the inspector walk in, he opened the medicine bottle, shook out a pill, put it in his mouth, took a sip of water, and said:

'You've ruined my career!'

Montalbano felt like laughing.

Apparently from the effort of screaming all those animal yells, the commissioner had lost his voice and now spoke like a horse-whisperer. 'I'm terribly sorry, Mr Commissioner, but—'

'Si . . . silence! I . . . I'll do the talking!'

But before starting to speak, Bonetti-Alderighi took another pill.

Then he opened and closed his mouth twice without saying anything. He was having trouble talking. 'I got a . . . call . . . earlier . . . from Dr Strangio, the pre . . . the president of the province . . . who told me that . . . that . . . you had . . . provoked his son . . . and had . . . him handcuffed . . .'

'But—'

'Ssshhh! And then . . . an hour ago . . . the Honourable Mongibello . . .'

Montalbano looked at him in fascination. The commissioner's voice now sounded all slurry, like that of someone dead drunk. It was like listening to Fiorello doing impersonations on the radio.

'. . . he informed me of his . . . decision . . . to . . . present a . . . request . . . in Parliament . . . on the part of his pa . . . party . . . for an investi . . . gation into the sui . . . cide of . . . Borselli . . . no . . .'

And he leaned back, against the headrest of the arm-chair, and said no more. Montalbano was worried. Was the commissioner dead? Had he fainted? The inspector circled round the desk, stood beside his boss, and bent down to listen to his breathing.

Bonetti-Alderighi had fallen asleep with his mouth open.

What to do? Wake him up? With four tranquillizers in his body, nobody was going to move him, not even with cannon blasts. He would be out until the next day.

Montalbano tiptoed out of the room, softly closing the door behind him.

'All cleared up,' he said to Dr Lattes, who looked at him questioningly in the waiting room.

FIVE

When he entered his office, he found Fazio there waiting for him.

'Any news?'

'Chief, I looked into the night-time surveillance of the Banca Regionale. They have a contract with something called the Sleep Easy Institution.'

'Well, give them a ring and—'

'Already taken care of. I just called them. On the night of the supermarket burglary the watchman on duty in the area was a certain Domenico Tumminello, but today's his day off.'

'You should ask for his number—'

'Already taken care of.'

Enough of this damn 'already taken care of'! What a pain! It set Montalbano's nerves on edge.

'Have you by any chance called him yet?'

'No, I didn't want to.'

'Why not?'

'Because I realized the poor man might still be asleep, since he's up all night.'

'Have you got his address?'

'Yes, sir. Salita Lauricella 12.'

'You know what? I think I'll go and see him myself, right now. If he's asleep, I'll let him sleep. Otherwise I want to talk to him.'

✳

Salita Lauricella 12 was a small three-storey building in a rather neglected state. The main door was open, and there was no intercom system.

He went in, and as there was no doorbell outside the first door he came to, he knocked. Absolute silence. He knocked harder, adding a couple of kicks as well.

'Who is it?' asked the voice of an elderly woman.

'Inspector Montalbano, police.'

'Whassatt? Talbano fleece? Talk louder, 'cause I'm a little deaf.'

'Inspector Montalbano, police!'

'Who do you want?'

'I'm looking for Mr Tumminello.'

'Who?'

'A little deaf' wasn't quite accurate. The lady wouldn't even have heard a naval battle in the port of Vigàta.

'I'm looking for Mr Tumminello!' Montalbano yelled.

'Parrinello?'

Luckily a woman of about forty stuck her head out over the banister on the landing above.

'Who are you looking for?'

'I'm looking for Domenico Tumminello.'

'I'm his wife. Come upstairs, sir, please come upstairs.'

Why did she sound so worried?

Montalbano didn't have time to climb the first of the three stairs before the woman came rushing down to him. He noticed that she was breathing heavily and looked scared out of her wits.

'What happened to my husband? What happened to him?'

'Don't be upset, signora. Nothing's happened to him. Is he not at home?'

'No, sir. But why are you looking for him?'

'I need some information from him. Do you know where I can find him at this hour?'

The woman didn't answer; two large tears rolled down her face.

She turned her back to him and started going upstairs.

Montalbano followed her. He found himself in a dining room, and the woman sat him down as she drank a glass of water.

'Signora, as you must have heard, I'm a police inspector. Can you tell me why you're so frightened?'

The woman sat down in turn, kneading her hands.

'Yesterday morning, Minico, my husband, got off work at six and came back here. He drank a little hot milk and then went to bed. I went out to do the shopping, and when I came back – it must have been around ten – the phone rang. The person said he was from the institution that Minico works for.'

'Did he tell you his name?'

'No, sir. He only said: "I'm from the institution." '

'Had you ever spoken to him before?'

'No, never.'

'OK, go on.'

'He said that Minico had to come to the institution at once because there was a client there who was complaining that Minico hadn't done his job right. He repeated that Minico should come at once, an' then he hung up.'

'And what did you do?'

'What was I supposed to do? I woke Minico up, tol' him about the phone call, and he got dressed, dead tired as he was, poor thing, and left.'

She started crying, heaving with sobs this time. Montalbano filled her glass with water and had her drink it. 'And what happened next?'

'I haven't seen 'im since.'

'He never came home? He never called? He didn't try to get in touch in any way?'

The woman shook her head. She was unable to speak.

'Does your husband own a car?'

She shook her head again.

'Listen, have you called the institution?'

'Of course. They deny everything . . . They say nobody called from there . . . an' no client complained . . .'

'Maybe he had an accident or got ill.'

The woman shook her head and pointed to a small table with a telephone and a phone book on it. 'All the hospitals,' she said. 'Nothing.'

Montalbano thought things over for a moment.

'Maybe it's best if you file a missing-persons report.'

She shook her head again forcefully.

'Why not?'

'Because if I file a missing-persons report he might go missing for sure.'

There was no countering this argument.

'Do you have a picture of your husband?'

The woman stood up with effort and left the room. She returned with an ID-format photo and handed it to the inspector. Then she sat back down, put her arms on the table, and laid her head in her arms.

Montalbano lightly stroked her hair and left.

*

As soon as he got back to the office, he called Fazio and told him what Tumminello's wife had said to him.

'The whole thing worries me,' said Fazio.

'Me too. But before we imagine the worst, I think it's best if you look into Tumminello's private life. Here, take his photo.'

Fazio looked at it. The photo showed a man of about

forty with an anonymous face: no moles, scars, nothing, one of those faces you forget barely five minutes after you've seen it.

'He doesn't look like a man with any troubles,' he said.

'Faces are deceptive, we know that from experience.'

Fazio went out and Augello came in. He was wearing a dark expression.

'What's wrong with you?'

'I'm still upset over that bastard Ragonese, I can't help it.'

'Then prepare for the worst.'

After Montalbano told him in great detail about his meeting with the commissioner, his facial expression turned even darker.

'So the eminent lawyer and honourable Member of Parliament Mongibello wants to bring a thing like that onto the floor?'

'It's understandable.'

'But what does he get out of it?'

'Are you kidding? It's the perfect excuse for him, Mimì! He's certainly not going to pass up an opportunity like this!'

'Explain what you mean.'

'There is no doubt that Mongibello will have the support of his own party, the majority party, in Parliament. There is no doubt that the Minister of the Interior, who is from a different party but is of the same ilk as his allies, will promise immediate action. And such action will mean, at the very least, the transfer of the commissioner and an early retirement for me. And you know what that means?'

'That you'll finally be out of everyone's hair.'

'That too, of course. But above all, it will mean a thousand points in the Cuffaro family's favour, and they'll come out of this stronger than ever before, with due thanks to the government.'

'But don't they realize this?'

'Some, maybe not; others, definitely.'

'Well, if anything like that happens, I'm going to resign,' said Mimì.

'Don't make me laugh. Let me ask you the same thing you asked me: what will you get out of that? You'll just add a few more points in the Mafia's favour. Whereas you need to keep fighting.'

'It's not easy, on two fronts.'

'*Two* fronts? Count them carefully. There are four.'

'Four?!'

'Yes indeed. One: common criminality; two: the occasional murder; three: the Mafia; four: the members of Parliament in collusion with the Mafia.'

'You know what I say? I say I resign right now.'

'And what'll you do?'

'I'll find something. I could get a job as a municipal police chief in a town somewhere.'

'Listen, between the time you put in a request and the time they accept you, you'll be probably over the hill. Therefore, in the meantime you'd better cover your back.

Draw up a report for the commissioner, straight away, so he can read it when he wakes up.'

'What should I write?'

'The facts. Everything from the moment you got to the supermarket; Borsellino's reactions to your questions; the inconsistencies in the execution of the burglary; my participation; everything. Without any commentary: just the facts.'

'OK.'

*

Not that he was worried about his career like the commissioner – who was practically on the verge of a stroke – since he, for his part, had pretty much reached the end. No, he was enraged; in fact, his blood was boiling.

In recent years, perhaps because of his increasing age, he was less and less able to control the disdain, and the subsequent feeling of rebellion, aroused in him by the more or less open support that a certain political formation, through the involvement of certain members of Parliament and senators, was always ready to provide the Mafia. And now they were even starting to pass a number of laws that hadn't the slightest thing to do with the law. What country was it where a minister had once said, while in office, that one had to learn to live with the Mafia? What country was it where a senator, convicted for first-degree collusion with the Mafia, had recycled himself and been re-elected? What country was it where a regional deputy, convicted for aiding and abetting Mafiosi, had risen to the rank of senator? What country was it where a man who'd been a minister and Prime Minister a great many times had been found definitively guilty of the crime of collusion with the Mafia, and yet continued to enjoy the status of senator for life?

The mere fact that these people never resigned of their own accord showed what sort of stuff they were made of.

He pushed away the plate in front of him.

'What? Aren't you going to eat?' Enzo asked him with concern.

'I'm suddenly not hungry any more.'

'Why not?'

'Too many worries.'

'Inspector, don't you know that worries are the worst enemies there are of your stomach and your cock, if you'll pardon my language?'

'But you can't always control what's going through your head. I'm sorry, because your pasta was magnificent.'

Even the customary stroll along the jetty to the lighthouse failed to dispel his bad mood.

*

'According to what everyone says, Tumminello has always been an honest, upstanding man,' Fazio began. 'Fired from his first job at thirty, he found his present stint as a night-watchman shortly afterwards, when a relative of his wife became one of the founding members of the security firm.

He's not known to have any secret girlfriends or other vices. He's a family man, all work and no play.'

'Listen, Fazio, I tried to persuade his wife to file a missing-persons report, but didn't succeed. You should try again yourself.'

'Already taken care of.'

God, what a pain!

'You went to see her?'

'Yes, sir.'

'How was she?'

'Desperate.'

'And what did she say to you?'

'She said she's too superstitious to file a missing-persons report. She's convinced that if she does, her husband really will disappear.'

'She said the same thing to me. So my question is: does she think her husband only pretended to disappear?'

Fazio threw up his hands.

'How do you see things?' the inspector asked him.

'I already told you. The whole thing looks really bad to me.'

'Meaning?'

'That as Tumminello was passing in front of the supermarket at that hour of the night, the poor bastard saw someone opening one of the doors . . .'

'But he wasn't worried because he recognized him,' Montalbano continued. 'It was someone belonging to the company that owns the supermarket.'

'Exactly. So he continues his rounds, completes his shift, and goes home to bed. When the burglar calls him at home and his wife wakes him up, the poor guy has no reason not to believe what the man says. He really thinks he's calling from the institution.'

'Also bear in mind that he still knows nothing about the robbery. Nobody's had any time to inform him yet.'

'Exactly. The minute he steps out of his house he finds the burglar there waiting for him. And he has no reason not to trust him. He may even have accepted his offer for a ride. And so he's fucked.'

'Poor guy,' was Montalbano's only comment.

After a moment of silence, Fazio spoke up: 'To conclude, if things are the way we think they are, this burglary has led to a murder and a suicide.'

'Two murders.'

Fazio stopped and stared at the inspector for a moment, speechless and open-mouthed. Then he got it.

'The manager!'

'Exactly.'

The inspector then told him everything he'd learned from Pasquano.

'There's something about this whole thing that doesn't convince me,' Fazio said at the end.

'What do you mean?'

'I think the total amount of money stolen from the supermarket comes to under twenty thousand euros.'

'So?'

'Isn't that a little skimpy to justify two murders?'

'What are you saying? Let me remind you first of all that people nowadays will kill just to snatch five hundred euros from a pensioner's hands. And secondly, don't forget that if it had been any other supermarket that had been robbed, I would certainly agree with you. But robbing the Cuffaros is another matter. If they catch you, you're dead, there's no getting around it.'

'That's true.'

Montalbano had an idea. But he didn't want to tell Fazio about it right away. He thought it over first, then made up his mind.

'Listen, tell me something: is the supermarket still closed?'

'Yes, until the day after tomorrow.'

'Do you know whether anyone's gone in after the suicide?'

'Who would go in? Tommaseo had the place sealed off at my request.'

Good man, Fazio!

'And do you know where Borsellino's copy of the keys ended up?'

'No. Probably in one of his pockets. His clothes are all at Dr Pasquano's lab at the institute.'

'Call him right now. Oh, and listen: don't speak directly to him – talk to his assistant. Otherwise Pasquano's liable to go ballistic and never stop. Call from here.'

The answer was yes: everything that belonged to Borsellino was still with Pasquano.

'Go there straight away, get everything, and bring it back to me here. I'll wait for you.'

'The clothes too?'

'The clothes too.'

*

At the Institute for Forensic Medicine, Fazio found Borsellino's shirt, vest, pants, socks, and shoes. In the trouser pockets they'd found a handkerchief, a set of keys, and nine euros in coins of different sizes.

'The jacket and tie are missing,' Fazio observed to Montalbano.

'I remember clearly that when he was hanging from the beam he wasn't wearing either. The killers must have taken them off the body, since you can't really hang yourself in a jacket and tie. You've got more freedom of movement in shirtsleeves.'

'So the jacket and tie should still be at the supermarket.'

'They almost certainly are. I think I even remember seeing them hanging in the office. But look at this shirt. Do you remember the one he was wearing when he called us about the burglary?'

'Yeah, I think it was dark blue.'

'I think so too. Whereas this one is white. Which means that there's no way that Borsellino, as they want us to believe, hanged himself as soon we left because he was upset over our interrogation. Pasquano's right. Borsellino went home, had a little something to eat – he wasn't very hungry, given all the worries he had on his mind – changed his shirt – remember how much he sweated in front of us? – and then went back to the supermarket.'

'Then he must've got a phone call, or a knock at the door, at which point he let his killers in.'

'Something like that,' said the inspector.

Then, looking Fazio in the eye, he added:

'Maybe we should go and have a look at the office.'

'We would need the prosecutor's authorization.'

'And what would I say to him? If Pasquano had written his doubts into the report, it would be easy . . .'

'Can I ask a question?'

'Of course.'

'Why didn't Pasquano want to mention the bruises?'

'He said it wouldn't stand up in court. But in my opinion he's just protecting himself.'

'From what?'

'My dear Fazio, do you somehow think that Pasquano, as well informed as he is, doesn't know that the Cuffaros are behind this whole affair? He must have decided that it wouldn't hurt to be a little careful.'

'So, you were saying?' Fazio asked.

'I was saying that since we've got nothing to show Tommaseo, I don't think it's such a good idea to go and stir him up.'

'You're right,' said Fazio, already knowing where the inspector wanted to go with this.

And indeed:

'You feel like coming with me tonight?'

'To the supermarket?'

'Where else do you think I'd want to go? Dancing?'

SIX

Fazio didn't hesitate for a second.

'OK.'

'Listen, to save time, I want you to do something for me. Go and see which of these keys open the front door to Borsellino's building and his apartment. So we don't waste time fumbling around in front of the supermarket. Then come by my place to pick me up around twelve-thirty, one o'clock.'

'Chief, the later it is, the better.'

'Then come by some time after one.'

But Fazio didn't get up from his chair.

'What is it?'

'Chief, you really need to think hard before doing something like this.'

'Meaning?'

'If they find out we entered the supermarket with no authorization, there could be some serious consequences.'

'Are you worried that the commissioner—'

'No, Chief, don't insult me. Nothing the commissioner says could ever make any difference to me.'

'And so?'

'I'm afraid that if anybody ever finds out – say, the Honourable Mongibello – they're liable to claim that we went into the supermarket to plant false evidence.'

'That you can bank on. But we'll make sure nobody ever finds out.'

*

Back at home he wolfed down another abundant helping of octopus. He had all the time in the world to digest. Then he cleared the table and went back out onto the veranda with a pack of cigarettes, half a glass of whisky, and a local newspaper. Naturally it featured an article about the supermarket burglary and the manager's suicide. The reporter seemed almost to have written the piece under dictation. He never mentioned the inspector's or Augello's names. Everything revolved around the central thesis that the shop's proceeds had been stolen by the manager himself, who, upon realizing he'd been found out, had hanged himself.

'Amen,' said Montalbano.

At midnight he turned on the television.

Pippo Ragonese, more purse-lipped than ever, was saying that even admitting that the manager himself robbed the shop, this did not justify Inspector Montalbano's brutal methods, which were the real reason the unfortunate Mr Borsellino had hanged himself.

'*Since when has a death sentence been the punishment for theft in our country?*' he asked rhetorically at one point.

'I'll tell you since when,' Montalbano answered. 'Ever since your government made it legal for people to shoot at thieves.'

He turned the television off and went and had a shower.

✶

At twelve-thirty, Livia rang.

'Sorry for calling so late, but I went to the movies with a friend. Were you already in bed?'

'No, I have to go out on a job.'

'At this time of the night?'

'At this time of the night.'

He heard her mutter something but couldn't understand what she said.

'What did you say?'

'Nothing.'

But the way she'd said 'nothing' let Montalbano know what she was thinking. And he flew into a rage.

'Livia, you continue to make a fuss over something we've discussed time and time again. I'm not some clerk with a fixed schedule. I don't get off work at five-thirty in the afternoon and go home. I—'

'Wait a second. What are you getting so worked up about?'

'Why shouldn't I get worked up? You're trying to insinuate that—'

'I'm not trying to insinuate anything. I asked you a simple question and you flew off the handle. You must admit, however, that you policemen have the best excuses for staying out all night.'

'Excuses?!'

'Yes, excuses. How could I ever verify that you're going out for work?'

'Verify?!'

'Stop repeating what I say, please.'

Montalbano started seeing red.

'And how could I ever verify that you were at the movies this evening with a friend?'

'So who would I have gone with, in your opinion?'

'How should I know? Maybe your little cousin, the one you spent a summer with on his boat!'

The spat was gargantuan this time.

*

Fazio arrived at quarter past one.

'Are we going in my car or yours?' he asked.

'Let's take yours.'

On their way there, the inspector said:

'When we were at the station I forgot to mention that you should find out what time the nightwatchmen normally pass by the supermarket.'

'Well, I didn't forget.'

Which was the exact equivalent of the damn 'already taken care of'. A simple variation on the theme.

Montalbano bit his lower lip to avoid reacting the wrong way. 'What did you find out?'

'That the nightwatchman checks the bank around one-thirty. He should already have come and gone by the time we get to the supermarket.'

'And when does he come by again?'

'An hour later.'

'We don't have a lot of time.'

'No need to worry. The office is at the back of the supermarket. The nightwatchman won't be able to see us back there.'

He was silent for a few moments and then said:

'I wanted to ask you something, Chief.'

'So go ahead.'

'What are you looking for in that office?'

'I'm not going there to search for anything.'

'Then what are we going there for?'

'I want to have another look at the office.'

Fazio didn't understand.

'But haven't you already seen it a hundred times?'

'I have, but always with different eyes.'

'Can you explain a little better?'

'When I went in there the first time, the office had been the scene of a burglary. So I looked at it as a place where a burglary had occurred. Then I went back there because it had been the scene of a suicide. And so I saw it as a place where someone had committed suicide. Later Pasquano told me that it was a murder, not a suicide, that had taken place there. But I haven't had a chance to look at it again from that perspective. That's what we're going to do now.'

*

Fazio parked two streets away.

'It's better if it isn't seen anywhere nearby.' Then, instead of heading for the four main metal rolling shutters, he turned the corner and made for the back of the supermarket.

'The back door is the service entrance, Chief. It's where they bring in the merchandise, where the cleaning ladies and staff enter. There aren't any streets running past it.'

This was true.

The back of the supermarket gave onto a large stretch of concrete that was fenced off and served as a parking area for delivery lorries.

Beyond the fence was the open countryside.

Fazio unstuck a part of the tape that held up the sheet of paper representing the police seal, then in the twinkling of an eye he opened the door, let the inspector in, followed him in, and closed the door behind them.

Walking in complete darkness towards the manager's office, at one point Montalbano stepped on a tin can and began skating along the floor, swearing like a madman and unable to stop his advance, finally crashing into a stack of little tubs of detergent, making a terrible racket.

Fazio came running and pulled him out from under a mountain of detergent tubs.

Perhaps owing to the powdered detergent, the inspector started sneezing so hard that his eyes began to water. And so the little he'd been able to see was no more. He took two steps with his arms extended before him like a blind man, then gave up.

'Help me.'

Fazio took him by the arm and led him all the way to the office.

There, he let him go and went and carefully closed all the rolling shutters, so that no light would filter outside. Then he turned on just the table lamp that was on the desk.

Now they could work with their minds at ease.

But as soon as he looked up at the inspector he couldn't keep from laughing.

Montalbano frowned.

'I'm sorry, Chief, but you look just like a fish covered in flour, ready for frying.'

Montalbano looked at his suit and shoes. They were all white. Apparently a few tubs of detergent had popped open in the crash.

He went into the office's small toilet and saw himself in the mirror. He looked like a clown. He washed his face and then went back and sat in the manager's chair.

He looked all around the room.

Just as he'd remembered, the jacket and tie were hanging from a hook on the wall beside the door.

'Search through the jacket pockets and give me everything you find.'

Borsellino apparently never used to keep anything on the desktop – no paper, no pens, none of the kinds of things that one might normally find on a desk.

Montalbano opened the middle drawer, the one that had been forced. The first time he'd looked in it he hadn't noticed, but this time he realized that in that drawer Borsellino kept everything he needed for writing: paper, pens, pencils, stamps, and so on. The telephone, on the other hand, sat on a small, separate table. Fazio, meanwhile, had put on the desk a wallet, five sheets of paper folded in four, and a small, empty book of matches of the sort that, in the days when you could smoke freely, without risk of fines or prison sentences, they used to give out at hotels, nightclubs, and restaurants. Inside were the words: *Chat Noir*.

'That's all I found, Chief.'

The wallet contained five hundred and fifty-five euros, a cash card and a national health service card, a credit card and ID card, a photo of a woman who must have been his deceased wife, and a receipt for a pair of glasses he was having repaired.

The sheets of paper were the accounts for incoming and outgoing merchandise.

Speaking of which, the inspector wondered, where did Borsellino keep his computer?

Montalbano opened the right-hand drawer and found the computer in it. Just under the edge of the desktop were some electrical sockets and a phone jack.

'Do you know what the Chat Noir is?' he asked Fazio.

'Yeah, it's a kind of "gentlemen's club" in Montelusa.'

'Frankly, Borsellino didn't seem the least bit like the kind of person who would frequent a place like that.'

'I agree.'

'So why do you think he had that book of matches in his pocket?'

'Well, there could be many explanations. Maybe somebody gave it to him.'

'But he didn't even smoke! What was he going to do with the matches?'

'Maybe he just put them in his pocket without thinking,' Fazio continued.

A second later, Montalbano smiled at him.

'Would you do me a favour? Look under the desk and see if you see an ashtray with a cigarette butt in it.'

Fazio lay face-down on the floor, because there was barely three inches of clearance between the bottom of the desk and the floor.

'Here it is,' he said, standing back up and putting the ashtray and butt on the desk. 'But how did you know . . .'

'I just imagined the scene.'

'Well, tell me how you did that.'

'OK: the killer enters the room with an accomplice, sits down, takes a cigarette out of the pack, and at the same time Borsellino takes an ashtray from the middle drawer and puts it down for him. The killer lights the cigarette with the last match and tosses the book onto the desk. Borsellino, who can't stand to see anything on his desk, grabs it automatically, just like you said, and puts it in his pocket. Then, in the struggle leading up to the hanging, the ashtray ends up under the desk. Make sense to you?'

'Makes sense.'

'Listen, put the butt and the empty book of matches in a plastic bag. They might turn out to be important.'

As Fazio was doing this, Montalbano suddenly thought of something else. 'So where'd the mobile end up?'

'What mobile?'

'Borsellino's.'

'But did he have one?'

'Of course he did. I distinctly remember that the first time I came here, he had it in his hand.'

'Search the drawers carefully.'

Montalbano reopened the middle one and stuck his hand all the way to the back. Pens, pencils, envelopes, letterhead paper, stamps, boxes of paper clips, rubber bands.

He opened the right-hand drawer. Just the computer.

He opened the left-hand drawer. Receipts, shipping forms, account books.

No mobile.

'Maybe the killers took it,' said Fazio.

'Or maybe he left it at home when he went back to eat and change his shirt.'

'It's possible,' said Fazio.

'And do you know what this means?'

'That we have to go to Borsellino's house,' sighed Fazio, resigned.

'Right on the money, Fazio. Put everything back in the jacket pockets and let's go.'

As Fazio was putting the wallet back, he gave a little cry.

'What is it?' the inspector asked.

'Maybe the mobile's here in the inside pocket. I forgot to look before.'

Fazio stuck two fingers in the specially made pocket and pulled out something that wasn't a mobile. It was an object shorter and fatter than a thermometer, but it wasn't a thermometer, because it was made of metal.

'What is it?' the inspector asked.

'Come on, Chief, you've seen hundreds of these things at press conferences! The journalists use them!'

'But what are they for?'

'They're digital recorders that you hook up to your computer. They're very sensitive and have large memories. But I don't know what they're called.'

'Let me see it.'

Fazio handed it to him, and Montalbano slipped it into his pocket.

'You know what I say? All things considered, let's take the computer too.'

Fazio rifled through the open drawer and after a few moments said:

'I'm ready.'

They went out of the office and straight into total darkness.

'Chief,' said Fazio, 'walk behind me with your hands on my shoulders. That way we won't do a repeat of before.'

Nobody saw them come out of the supermarket.

And they didn't run into anyone on their way to the car.

*

As they drew near to Borsellino's place, Fazio again parked in a nearby street, but not too close. By now, however, it was the middle of the night, and the only souls about were a couple of dogs and three cats squabbling near a rubbish bin. Before getting out of the car, Fazio took two torches and gave one to the inspector.

'Borsellino lived on the fifth floor,' he said as they headed off.

'Is there a lift?' Montalbano asked, worried.

'Yes there is. What should we do?'

'What do you mean?'

'Should we go up to the sixth floor and come down one, or to the fourth and go up one?'

'I like the first one better,' said the inspector.

Fazio opened the building's main door as if he'd always

lived there himself. But at the door to the apartment, he had some trouble.

'What's the matter?'

The key refused to go into the lock.

He tried again.

'What is this?' he said under his breath. 'Just a few hours ago it opened just fine!'

At last he succeeded, and they went in and shut the door behind them. They turned on their torches.

The apartment consisted of a small entranceway, four rooms off a central corridor, two bathrooms, and a kitchen. Apparently Borsellino, since his wife's death, had not had any other women living with him. The place was in perfect order.

The mobile was neither in the bedroom nor in the dining or living room. Nor in the kitchen or bathroom.

The last room was a sort of study.

There was a desk identical to the one in the supermarket, with an armchair and pair of metal filing cabinets full of binders. No mobile anywhere to be seen.

Montalbano opened the desk's three drawers one after the other and was immediately convinced they contained no mobile.

But there was something that didn't add up. And all of a sudden he realized what it was.

Just under the edge of the desktop, above the right-hand drawer, were the electrical sockets and phone jack necessary for using a computer. But there was no computer on the desk.

Fazio, who'd been following the inspector's movements attentively, immediately understood.

'It's possible he didn't have a computer at home. These desks are ready-made for computers, so it doesn't mean . . .'

Montalbano moved a few papers that were on the desk, and from underneath them appeared a mouse and a keyboard. He showed them to Fazio without saying anything.

Fazio suddenly slapped himself on the forehead and ran to the entranceway. The inspector followed him.

Fazio opened the door softly and tried to put the key in the lock. It encountered resistance again.

'It's been forced,' he said. 'Somebody came in and—'

'Made off with the computer,' Montalbano concluded.

'But the weird thing is that they definitely did it after I tested the key earlier,' said Fazio. 'When we were at the supermarket. And it's possible that—'

'Right now they're at the supermarket to get the other computer, because they don't know that we've already got it,' Montalbano concluded again. 'It's like we're taking turns.'

'What should we do? Pay them a visit?' Fazio suggested.

'Let's.'

*

They sped to the supermarket. On the way there, Fazio asked:

'Are you armed?'

'No. Are you?'

'I am. There's a wrench in the glove compartment. You should take it. It's better than nothing.'

It wasn't the first wrench he'd had to deal with recently, he thought as he slipped it into his jacket pocket.

'First we'll go past the main entrance and see if there are any cars parked outside,' said Fazio.

There were no cars. Fazio drove carefully to the area behind the supermarket. There were no cars there, either.

When they got out, the first thing they saw were the police seals on the ground. Fazio had put them back when they'd gone out, of that he was certain.

So there was someone inside the supermarket, or else there had just been someone.

SEVEN

They had their confirmation that someone had been there after them when this key, too, had a lot of trouble fitting into the lock.

At last the key turned, but contrary to Montalbano's expectations, Fazio did not open the door right away, but turned and looked at him.

'So?'

'Let's make a deal first,' said Fazio.

'Let's hear it.'

'I'll go in, but you won't.'

'Why?'

'Because you're not armed.'

'But I've got the wrench!'

'You can just imagine how scared they'll be when they see you've got a wrench. I'd bet the family jewels that the men in there are the same ones who've already killed two people.'

'Listen to me for a second, Fazio. There's no way I'm

waiting outside! And don't forget that I give the orders around here!'

'Chief, with all due respect, just think for a second. It's so dark in there you can't take a single step. You can't even see an inch in front of you. And if you run into another stack of detergent, they'll blow us away before we can say "boo".'

Humiliated and offended, but realizing that Fazio was right, he didn't know what to say.

'All right?'

'All right,' Montalbano promised, swallowing the bitter pill.

Fazio took out his pistol, cocked it, opened the door, and went in.

Montalbano closed the door most of the way and peered through the crack. But he couldn't see a thing. Total blindness. And it was all surely the fault of ageing. On top of everything else, he couldn't hear anything either, because Fazio moved like a cat.

Barely five minutes had gone by when Fazio reappeared.

'They were here, but they're gone.'

'How could you tell they were here?'

'They left all the doors of the cupboard open, as well as the desk drawers. They were looking for the computer. Good thing we were able to get it first.'

*

When he got home he showered to wash away the powdery detergent that had entered through his shirt collar and sifted down over his shoulders and chest. It took a good while because upon coming into contact with the water, the detergent bubbled up worse than soap.

When he got into bed he smelled like fresh laundry. But he was unable to fall asleep.

A question kept spinning insistently in his head: why did Borsellino have a recorder like that in his jacket pocket?

Of course he didn't always keep it there. He must have been in the habit of putting it in his pocket after using it.

But what did he do with it? Record music?

No, he didn't seem like the type who would listen to Chopin or Brahms.

He didn't seem like the type for opera, either. Or even pop songs.

Therefore it was clear that, now and then, he must have recorded what was said in his office.

For what purpose?

He probably turned on the recorder when he had to reprimand or actually sack an employee. That way, if there was a dispute afterwards, he could always show what had actually happened.

Satisfied with the explanation he'd come up with, Montalbano fell asleep.

*

Early in the morning, he had a dream.

And he remembered it because he woke up right in the middle, and it was therefore still fresh in his memory.

In the dream he'd been watching part of an American movie he'd seen a long time before. It was called *The Invincibles*. No, he was wrong. The film was called *The Untouchables*.

It was about the war a special police unit was waging against the famous Al Capone. And there was a scene that he'd really liked a lot, the one where they arrest Al Capone's accountant on an enormous staircase at the railway station.

It was very important to nab the mysterious accountant because from his records they could prove that the boss was dodging his taxes.

The funny thing about the dream was that in that scene, he, Montalbano, was the top cop, and Fazio was his assistant.

What happens in the film is that, just as the two policemen are taking aim at the accountant's bodyguard, a pram with a child inside slips away from the woman who is pushing it and starts tumbling down the stairs. The image was clearly a homage to the great Soviet filmmaker Sergei Eisenstein.

Since, in the dream, Montalbano wasn't paying homage to anyone, there was no pram, but in its place there was a tub of detergent not with a baby inside, but with Borsellino the manager in swaddling clothes, bonnet, and glasses, crying desperately and calling for help on his mobile.

Fazio tried to stop the detergent pram but was unable, and the detergent tub with Borsellino inside ended up squashed under a train pulling into the station.

Meanwhile the accountant's bodyguards were throwing tins of tomatoes at Montalbano. One of them hit him in the forehead and cracked open. Fazio, seeing all that red streaming from his head, was scared to death.

'Inspector, you're wounded!'

'No! It's just tomatoes! Have you forgotten we're in a film?'

A royal shambles, in short.

Then he remembered that before going out on his night raid with Fazio, he'd wolfed down a hefty plate of that damn octopus.

That explained the whole bloody jumble of his dream. He'd had trouble digesting.

*

He woke up only because he'd set the alarm clock. He felt completely muddle-headed. He hadn't slept even three hours. Just to be safe, the first thing he did was to take the rest of the octopus still in the fridge and put it outside, on the veranda. The cats could feast on it.

Then he had a very long shower, more to wake himself up than to wash. And he only stopped because he was afraid to use up all the water in the tanks.

Finally he put on a clean suit. The one from the day before was too powdery, and he'd already put it into the laundry basket. Adelina would see to having it properly cleaned.

He was about to go out when the phone rang.

Oh, God! he thought. Please spare me the usual morning murder! I'm in no condition to investigate anything, even though I'm alive!

But it was Livia.

'How are you?'

Where had he read that that was a question one should never ask anyone?

'Not too bad. And you?'

'I didn't sleep because of you.'

'Because of me?'

'Yes. Since we hung up last night on a bad note, I wanted to . . . apologize. I called you every half-hour. But you didn't answer. At three o'clock I stopped calling, but I was upset. Why didn't you answer?'

'Livia, my precious darling, try to think for a second, and then answer me this: what, in your opinion, did we quarrel about?'

'I don't remember.'

'Let me refresh your memory. We quarrelled because you got upset that I had to go out on a job. Remember now?'

'Vaguely.'

The woman was going to drive him out of his mind!

'So, to conclude: since I was out of the house, I couldn't answer your calls. Elementary, my dear Watson.'

'Ha ha ha!'

'What's that supposed to mean: ha ha ha?'

'It means, in other words, that if you call me Watson, you think you're Sherlock Holmes!'

No, a spat first thing in the morning, no!

'*Ciao*, Livia, talk to you this evening. Now I really have to run.'

'Run, run!'

God, that woman was obnoxious sometimes!

*

'Cat, did Fazio by any chance give you a computer?'

'Yessir, Chief, 'e did, iss in my custidy. Couldja tell me wha' I'm asposta do witta foresaid?'

'Open it, look at everything that's in it — and I mean everything — and then come to me and give me a synopsis.'

Catarella looked distressed.

'What's wrong?'

'I din't unnastand the seccun ting I'm asposta give yiz.'

'What thing?'

''At ting ya said. The synappsus.'

'Cat, I mean just come and tell me what's inside that computer.'

'Ah, good, Chief. Ya 'ad me scared f'r a minnit.'

*

Fazio came in.

'Any news?'

'Nah.'

'What about Augello?'

'An attempted burglary was reported last night at a furrier's, and Inspector Augello went to check it out.'

'Let's hope he isn't later accused of driving the furrier to suicide.'

'I don't think there's any danger this time, Chief. The shop belongs to a man named Alfonso Pirrotta, who's one of those people who refuse to pay the protection money.'

'So the attempted burglary must be a warning to him to pay up,' said Montalbano. Then he asked: 'How many people are there in Vigàta who don't pay?'

'Right now, about thirty. But their number may increase soon. There's a new judge in Montelusa, Barrafato, who says exactly what he thinks, and the shop owners are feeling encouraged.'

'Poor Barrafato!'

Fazio gave him a perplexed look.

'Why do you say that?'

'Because sooner or later, if he gets under the Mafia's skin enough, Barrafato will find himself summonsed by the high council of the magistrature for some phone tapping that, in the opinion of some Member of Parliament, he wasn't authorized to do, and his name will be plastered all over the newspapers and TV, and he'll end up transferred for being incompatible with his present environment. How much you want to bet?'

'Nothing. I don't like to lose bets.'

✳

Fazio returned a short while later with a little grin on his face that the inspector didn't like one bit.

'Shall we have another go at it, Chief?'

'Another go at what?'

'At signing documents.'

Montalbano weighed his options. Since he had nothing else to do, it was better to brave the agony.

'All right, bring me ten or so.'

*

He'd just finished reading and signing half of the documents when the telephone rang. He looked at his watch: it was almost eleven. He picked up the phone with great enthusiasm – maybe something had happened that would spare him the tremendous pain in the arse of signing more papers. It was Catarella.

'Chief, 'at'd be 'at jinnelman from th' udder day 'at wants a talk t'yiz poissonally in poisson.'

'What do you mean, the "gentleman from the other day"? Did he tell you his name?'

'Yeah, Chief, 'is name is Strangio.'

Strangio?! Giovanni Strangio? The crazy motorist?

It wasn't possible. Catarella, as usual, had got the name wrong.

'Are you sure his name is Strangio?'

'Crass my 'eart, Chief.'

By now his heart must have more crosses than a cemetery.

And what could Strangio want?

Before receiving him, however, it was better to make sure it was indeed him.

'Listen, show him into the waiting room. Oh, hang on. As you're showing him in, try and see if he's carrying a wrench.' Just to be safe.

Catarella came back to the phone after a brief spell.

'Y'know wha' I did, Chief? I pretinnit to slip, an' to keep fro' fallin' I grabbed right onto the guy, so I cou' check 'im out. Pretty good idea, eh, Chief?'

'Well done, Cat, my compliments. But did he have a wrench?'

'Nah, 'e din't. Crass my 'eart.'

But the inspector wasn't convinced.

He let a few minutes go by, got up, left the room, and walked past Catarella, putting his finger to his lips to signal to him to keep quiet, went to the main entrance, and stuck his head out, scanning the car park.

The BMW he knew well was there.

There was therefore no doubt that it was him.

Again he walked past Catarella, who was looking at him in bewilderment and standing at attention, went back into his office, and picked up the phone.

'Cat, get me Fazio, would you?'

He had just time to count up to five.

'What is it, Chief?'

'Listen, Fazio, that motorist is here, Strangio, the man I arrested the other day, the one who was a little too upset and—'

'I heard about the incident, Chief, but I've never seen this Strangio in person.'

'It doesn't matter, you'll see him now. Since I'm not sure how he feels about things at the moment, it might be best if you were also present for my meeting with him.'

'I'm on my way.'

Better to be on one's guard with a character like that.

Fazio came in and sat down in one of the two chairs in front of the desk.

Montalbano rang Catarella and told him to bring in the man who wanted to talk to him.

At the mere sight of him, Montalbano was speechless.

The guy who came in was not the Giovanni Strangio he'd met, but a sort of twin brother.

As much as the first one was dissolute, neurotic, and threatening, this one was polite, orderly, and composed.

'Good morning,' he greeted them.

'Please sit down,' said Montalbano, gesturing towards the empty chair.

Strangio sat down.

'May I smoke?' he asked.

'Actually, it's not allowed,' said the inspector. 'But we can make an exception.'

Wasn't it well known that you're supposed to humour the insane?

Strangio pulled out his pack and lighter and lit a cigarette.

At that moment both the inspector and Fazio noticed

that the young man's hands were trembling violently. Apparently he was having trouble controlling the powerful agitation he felt inside.

Montalbano exchanged a lightning-quick glance with Fazio, communicating to him to stay on the alert.

It was best not to force the young man to speak; he should be allowed all the time he needed.

'I'm here . . . I've come to report a murder,' Strangio said suddenly.

The effect was the same as if he had thrown a bomb into the middle of the room.

Fazio jumped straight up; Montalbano stiffened against the back of his chair.

'The murder of whom?' the inspector ventured to ask.

'My . . . my girlfriend,' the young man replied.

Montalbano and Fazio were barely breathing.

'Her name is . . . was . . . Mariangela Carlesimo.'

He took a last drag on his cigarette.

'Where can I throw this away?' he asked, holding up the cigarette butt.

The question dispelled the tension.

Montalbano relaxed, and Fazio said:

'Give it to me.'

And he went and threw it out of the window.

'I didn't kill her, of course,' Strangio resumed. 'I merely found the body. And on top of that—'

'Just a minute,' Montalbano said, cutting him off. 'Don't say any more. Please, don't go any further.'

The young man looked at him questioningly. As did Fazio.

'You see, the fact is that it was I who arrested you and charged you over the incident the other day.'

'So what?'

'It means that I may not be the most suitable person to deal with any crime in which you are in some way involved.'

'Why not?'

'Because I might be accused of handling the case in a – how shall I say? – less than impartial way. Have I made myself clear?'

'Quite clear. And so?'

'And so I'll be even more explicit. Have you already talked about this with Nero Duello the lawyer?'

'Yes, sir, I have. He's the first person I told about it.'

'And the second was your father?'

It just slipped out. He could have bitten his tongue. The young man, however, didn't notice the provocation.

'Naturally.'

'And what did the lawyer tell you?'

'To report to you just the same.'

'Why didn't he come with you?'

'He was busy in court.'

Fazio couldn't hold out any longer.

'What do you intend to do?' he asked the inspector.

'Where is the victim?' Montalbano asked Strangio in turn.

'In our house. We'd been living together for a while.'

'Let's go,' said the inspector, standing up.

'Shall I inform Forensics, the prosecutor, and Dr Pasquano?' Fazio asked.

Montalbano was about to say yes, then stopped in his tracks.

Wouldn't it be better to wait and make sure that there actually was a dead woman's body in the house? Wasn't it also possible that this madman had made the whole thing up?

'Call them when I tell you to.'

'You don't want to know anything else?' the young man asked in surprise.

'What you've already told me is enough. If you have anything else to say, I'd rather you save it for the prosecutor.'

'As you wish. Shall we go in my car?' Strangio asked.

And end up crashing into a tree?

'No, we'll go in a patrol car. Is Gallo around?'

'Yes, sir.'

Fazio went to get Gallo. Montalbano and Strangio exited the station to wait for the patrol car. The young man lit another cigarette.

Montalbano was watching him out of the corner of his eye, because Strangio's body now seemed to be quaking all over, as if he had an electric current running through him.

Then everything happened at once.

EIGHT

As soon as the patrol car appeared with Gallo driving, Strangio tossed aside his cigarette, took a big leap forward, and dived into its wheels.

Luckily the car was already pulling up and therefore moving slowly.

As a result, Strangio did not succeed in getting run over. He only banged his head hard against the bumper and lay stretched out on the ground, blood gushing out of his forehead like a fountain.

Fazio and Montalbano crouched down to look at him. At first glance, it didn't look like anything serious.

Gallo ran back into the station. Strangio started crying. Gallo returned with disinfectant and cotton and tried to staunch the bleeding.

But it was useless. The wound was too big.

'Take him to A&E,' said Montalbano. 'Then come back here and get me.'

*

Instead of going straight back into his office, he preferred to stay outside and smoke a cigarette. He wasn't the least bit upset by Strangio's gesture. He immediately knew it was not an impulsive act prompted by sorrow, despair, remorse, or God knows whatever other motive.

No, it was a gesture made with a lucid mind, conceived and calculated down to the last millimetre. Strangio at that moment was not out of his head, even if that's what he wanted it to look like. His intention was apparently to achieve a certain effect. But what?

His act was a gesture typical of a guilty person wanting to appear innocent. It was like putting his personal signature on the murder. He would now claim that he threw himself in front of the car out of despair over losing his girlfriend.

But the inspector decided to stop thinking about it; otherwise he would end up having preconceived ideas.

He went into his office.

And just to force himself not to think about anything, he resumed signing those damn documents.

✳

Fazio came in about an hour later.

'How'd it go?'

'They gave him five stitches.'

'And where is he now?'

'Just outside, in the car.'

'Is he in any condition to—'

'Listen to me, Chief: aside from a little headache, he's perfectly fine.'

As soon as they went out, Montalbano saw Gallo with a bucket of water and a sponge, heading for the car.

'What are you doing?'

'I want to wash the bumper. It's got blood on it.'

'Wait a second. Do we have a Polaroid?'

'No. But I've got a good camera.'

'That's even better. Go get it and take some pictures of the car. Then you can wash it.'

'Would you explain to me why?' Fazio asked.

'Because Strangio is capable of anything, even saying that we broke his head ourselves inside the station to make him confess that he was the murderer.'

There was nothing to be done about it. He had deeply rooted prejudices against the kid. However well founded.

Better pass the case on to someone else as soon as the opportunity arose.

*

Strangio lived in a small detached two-storey house at Via Pirandello, number 14. The street was a bit outside of town and ran parallel to the main road that Montalbano took to go to Marinella and back.

Practically attached to the house on the right, but separated by a small alley that could barely fit a car, was a seven-storey building. There wasn't anyone looking out, except for a woman of a certain age enjoying the sun on her balcony.

Luckily nobody knew about the murder yet.

An open gate gave onto a driveway that cut through a small, poorly tended garden with more weeds than flowers. The driveway went as far as the back of Strangio's house.

Fazio parked right outside the gate, and they all got out.

'You lead the way,' Montalbano said to Strangio.

They went down the driveway and came to the front door. Strangio, who had the keys in his pocket, slipped a key in the lock, but hesitated for a moment before turning it. Then he made up his mind and opened the door, stepping quickly aside.

'Do I have to go in first?' he asked.

'Yes.'

'I don't feel up to it,' he said firmly, bringing a hand to his bandaged head.

He was as pale as a corpse.

'Would you rather wait outside?' Montalbano asked him.

'If possible . . .'

'Just tell me one thing, I'm curious. Why did you choose to come to the station to inform us, instead of simply making a phone call after you discovered the body?'

Strangio swallowed; his mouth was probably dry.

'I don't know . . . my first reaction was to run as far as possible away from here.'

'All right. Gallo, you stay here with him. Where is it?'

'Where's what?' asked Strangio, confused.

'The body.'

'Upstairs, in the study.'

On the ground floor were the dining room, living room, kitchen, and a bathroom. A nice wooden staircase led upstairs. They went up.

Here there was a large master bedroom with the bed in disorder, a guest room, a bathroom, and the study.

The whole upstairs was permeated with the sickly sweet smell of blood, a smell that Fazio and Montalbano knew well, which clung to one's throat like a nauseating taste.

Lying across the desk in the study was the body of a young woman, completely naked with legs spread. She had very long blonde hair and must have been quite beautiful.

She'd been slaughtered; there was no other word for it.

Her body was one giant wound. The killer had lashed out with such fury against her breasts and lower abdomen that you could see the insides of her rent flesh.

The blood had formed an enormous puddle on the floor. It was impossible to get near without stepping in it.

Montalbano couldn't take any more.

'Alert everyone,' he said, leaving the room.

Now he understood why Strangio hadn't wanted to come upstairs with them.

He went downstairs, leaned out of the doorway, and called Gallo and Strangio. The three of them went into the living room to wait.

Nobody spoke until Forensics arrived.

✻

Then, immediately afterwards, Dr Pasquano arrived.

He'd come with the ambulance and the two stretcher-bearers who would take the body to the Institute for Forensic Medicine for the post-mortem. He had a dark look on his face and didn't greet anyone.

He must have lost at poker the previous evening.

'Where is it?'

'Upstairs,' Fazio replied.

Pasquano disappeared and then reappeared a minute later, now red in the face and angrier than before.

'What is this shit? They told me I had to wait another half an hour! They're amusing themselves taking pictures! As if there was any use for them! And I haven't got any time to waste!'

He sat down furiously in the armchair beside the one the inspector was sitting in, pulled a newspaper out of his coat pocket, and started reading.

But since Montalbano happened to crane his neck to have a better look at a headline, the doctor, after giving him a dirty look, went and sat in a chair further away.

Gallo was staring straight ahead, Strangio had his head in his hands, Pasquano was reading and muttering to himself, while Fazio, who'd come downstairs after Forensics arrived, was looking at a piece of paper.

Montalbano felt as if he was in a dentist's waiting room. He got up and went out into the little garden to smoke a cigarette.

A few minutes later Fazio joined him.

'Chief, could you please tell me why you won't interrogate Strangio?'

'It would be a waste of time.'

'Why?'

'I'm convinced that the commissioner, as soon as he regains consciousness, will take the case away from me. And this time he'll be fairly right to do so.'

'Is that the only reason?'

Fazio was an intelligent person, as he was showing with that question.

'Fazio, you can work out the other reasons yourself.'

'Are you worried they're setting a trap for you?'

'In a way, yes. If at some point they come out with the story that I had ulterior hostile motives in Strangio's regard, then the results of my investigation could easily be invalidated.'

At that moment Prosecutor Tommaseo arrived with Deluca, the court clerk.

'I apologize for being late. I had a little mishap with the car.'

Tommaseo not only wore thick glasses that looked like bulletproof glass, he drove like a drunken dog. There wasn't a single thing along whatever road he was travelling – tree, rubbish bin, pole, what have you – that he might not crash into. And since he always drove at thirty kilometres an hour, all he ever damaged was his car.

'Who's the victim?' he asked Montalbano.

'A very young, very beautiful woman.'

As Tommaseo's eyes started to sparkle, the inspector threw down his ace.

'Completely naked.'

'Was she raped?'

'Probably.'

Tommaseo darted for the door and disappeared inside the house in the twinkling of an eye.

'Follow him,' Montalbano said to Fazio, 'and when he starts questioning Strangio, let me know. I want to be present.'

✻

The young man's deposition was taken by Tommaseo and written down by the clerk in the living room. Fazio was present, and Gallo was asked to step outside.

As was Dr Pasquano – who went swearing into the dining room.

'Name, address, date of birth.'

Strangio complied.

Upon hearing the young man's surname, Tommaseo hesitated for a moment.

'Are you by any chance the son of—'

112

'Yes, my father's the president of the province.'

'I see,' said Tommaseo.

He heaved a sigh and continued:

'Tell me how you discovered the murder.'

The young man must have regained his self-control. Now he seemed actually relaxed; his hands had even stopped trembling. Maybe the bump on the head and loss of blood had done him good.

'When I got into Punta Raisi airport this morning . . .'

'Where were you coming from?'

'Rome.'

'What were you doing in Rome?'

'Working.'

'You work in Rome?'

'No, I work here, but I had to go to Rome for a meeting.'

'Who's your employer?'

'Ugotti. They make computers, printers, that kind of thing . . . But I'm not a normal employee. I'm the company's sole representative in Sicily. Every month there's a meeting in Rome of all the representatives. It lasts one day, and the date changes each month, though it's always during the first week.'

'So you were in Rome all day yesterday?'

'Yes.'

'At what time did you leave Palermo?'

'Yesterday? I took the seven-thirty morning flight.'

'OK, go on.'

'When I landed in Palermo this morning on the nine o'clock flight, which got in on time, I went and got my car, which I'd left the previous day in the car park, and headed straight back to Vigàta. But . . .'

'But?'

'I felt uneasy. Something didn't seem right.'

'And why was that?'

'Well, normally, whenever I come into Punta Raisi, I call Mariangela, my girlfriend. I did the same thing this morning, but there was no answer. I called repeatedly from the car as I was driving back. She never answered. So I was worried.'

'Why? She might just have gone out to buy groceries or for some other reason.'

'Mariangela never got up before ten o'clock.'

'She could have gone to see her parents.'

'They don't live in Vigàta.'

'Did you call her mobile or her land line?'

'I called the land line. One phone is on the nightstand right beside the bed. I let it ring a long time.'

'Why didn't you try her mobile?'

'Because Mariangela keeps . . . used to keep it turned off until she got up. On top of that, she knew I was going to call her as usual, as soon as I got in, and so . . .'

'Go on.'

'When I got home, I put the car in the garage, which is behind the house, and I entered the house through the garden. I opened the door and called out, but there was no answer. I thought maybe she was still sound asleep. She sometimes takes sleeping pills. So I went upstairs and went into the bedroom. She wasn't there. I went into the hallway and from there I saw something . . . something terrible on the desk in the study. I took one step and . . . and that's all.'

'So you never went into the study?'

'No.'

'Why not?'

'Well . . . partly because my legs wouldn't move . . . partly because I realized that there was nothing I could do by that point . . . And then . . . because I just couldn't believe it. I don't know how else to put it . . .'

'How did you know she was dead?'

For the first time Strangio raised his eyes and looked at Tommaseo, as though shocked.

'Good God, it was perfectly obvious!'

'What was your girlfriend's name?'

'Mariangela Carlesimo; she was twenty-three years old and was studying architecture at the University of Palermo.'

'How long had you been together?'

'Together, over a year and a half. But we moved here about six months ago.'

At this point Montalbano got up and went out.

'Gallo, take me to Enzo's.'

There was no point in staying any longer to listen to Tommaseo's questions. It was better to go and eat.

Outside the gate there were television crews and news-papermen who had descended on the scene like flies drawn to shit.

*

He didn't give Enzo the satisfaction his dishes deserved. He ate little, and listlessly at that.

He had no explanation for his malaise.

Was it perhaps because he couldn't get the sight of that poor girl's hacked-up body out of his mind? Or was it because Strangio's whole attitude seemed fishy to him?

The customary stroll along the jetty was more a way to pass the time than a digestive necessity.

*

Back at the office, the first thing he did was to call the commissioner. Lattes answered the phone and told him the commissioner was still indisposed, but that Deputy Commissioner Concialupo was replacing him in all respects for the time being. If the inspector had anything urgent to discuss, he should address the deputy commissioner.

But Montalbano didn't feel like talking to Concialupo, who was perfectly nice but had to be told things three times before he understood them.

'Dr Lattes, do you know when the commissioner—'

'Surely tomorrow morning, with God's help.'

What to do?

The best thing was not to have anything to do directly with Strangio until he'd spoken to the commissioner.

Questioning him before that would be a mistake.

*

The telephone rang.

'Chief, onna phone I got the proxecutor onna phone.'

'Tommaseo?'

'Poissonally in poisson.'

'Put him through.'

'But did you see what a gorgeous girl she was?' Tommaseo began.

What a surprise! He must be drooling at the other end. Whenever a beautiful young woman was murdered, a crime of passion committed, or amorous intrigues figured in the background of a case, Tommaseo was in his element.

The inspector's own theory was that it was a sort of compensation for the fact that the prosecutor was not known to have ever had any kind of relations with a woman.

'I have her photos here in front of me, and I'm telling you, when she was alive she was a rare beauty,' Tommaseo continued.

Montalbano was horrified.

But what photos was he looking at? The hair-raising photos of the corpse?

'Did you get them from Forensics?'

'No! I asked Strangio for them. By the way, I've formed a pretty clear idea of things, you know.'

Montalbano was stunned.

Never mind Sherlock Holmes! Tommaseo was a combination of Poirot, Maigret, Marlowe, Carvalho, Derrick, Columbo, and Perry Mason all thrown together in a blender.

'You don't say!'

'I certainly do, my friend! Listen, I'll tell you how the whole thing went. I'm absolutely sure of it, cross my heart.'

As Catarella had said. With the result that somebody's heart was going to give out sooner or later.

'Please enlighten me.'

'It's really quite simple. I'm convinced that when Strangio went back home unexpectedly, he found his girlfriend in the midst of sexual congress with another man. And so, insane with jealousy, he killed her.'

But how could Tommaseo not have noticed that the girl's blood was already dry? That she'd been murdered the previous day, at the very least? Montalbano decided to toy with him a little.

'But how did you manage, in such a short time . . . ?' he asked, feigning amazement and admiration.

'Just talking to him was enough. Anyway, you were there yourself, weren't you? Did you see what self-control? What pitiless lucidity, I might add?'

'What self-will!' said Montalbano.

'Exactly. What? The girl you live with gets murdered and you don't bat an eyelid?'

'Don't even wince?' said Montalbano.

'Exactly. You don't even twitch?'

'Don't shed a tear?' Montalbano suggested.

'Exactly. So you agree, Montalbano, that such coldness is typical of a murderer?'

'Absolutely.'

'So I want you to put the screws on him, I mean it!'

'But is he under arrest?'

'No. You tell me: how could I? For the moment he's simply a witness.'

And therefore should be treated like one. So much for the screws.

NINE

An hour later Fazio came in.

'You know what? Tommaseo phoned me,' said the inspector.

'What did he want?'

'He wants us to put the screws on Strangio.'

'Ha ha ha!'

'Why do you laugh?'

'Because he himself was very careful not to put the screws on him! Didn't you see how his expression changed when Strangio told him whose son he was? Mr Prosecutor wants us to be his lightning rod!'

'But,' said Montalbano, 'that doesn't mean we shouldn't carry on just the same. Taking care that none of it reaches Strangio's ears or his father's. Otherwise things could get dangerous.'

'Like touching the third rail,' said Fazio.

'The girl — what's her name? — ah, yes, Mariangela Colosimo . . .' the inspector began.

'Carlesimo,' Fazio corrected him.

How was it that he never used to get people's names wrong but now was becoming more and more like Catarella?

'This girl,' he resumed with a note of pique in his voice, 'based on what her boyfriend said, did not seem like the housekeeping type. She must certainly have had a cleaning lady she paid by the hour. We should find out who she is, what her name is—'

'Already taken care of,' said Fazio.

The inspector saw red.

Overcome by a rage as unreasonable as it was irresistible, he slammed his hand on the desk.

Surprised, Fazio gave a start.

'What was that?'

'Nothing,' said Montalbano, ashamed of his nervous outburst. 'I killed a fly that was bothering me. So tell me.'

'Can I look at a piece of paper I have in my pocket?' Fazio asked in a tone that was at once prefatory and slightly combative.

'Provided there's nothing from the records office.'

'Fine. After everything had been done at Strangio's house and everyone had just left, I was getting into the car to come back here when a woman of about fifty came up to me, wanting to know what had happened. I told her she would find out on the TV news. But then she said she was Strangio's housekeeper, and that she normally came in to work at one. And so I told her what happened, and since she could hardly walk after hearing the news, Gallo and I gave her a ride home. That way I was able to question her eye to eye.'

'Well done, Fazio.'

'Thanks.'

Only now did he pull the piece of paper out of his pocket. He gave it a quick glance and then put it back in his pocket.

'The housekeeper's name is Concettina Vullo. She used to work every day except Sunday. She would come in at one and stay until four. She cooked, ironed, and cleaned.'

'What did she tell you about Strangio?'

'She said she didn't know him well because he almost always ate out during the day. She said he was flighty.'

'Flighty? Meaning?'

'He'd be cheerful one minute and then totally pissed off the next.'

'Did she ever witness any quarrels between him and his girlfriend?'

'No.'

'And what was the girl like?'

'Basically a nice girl. She would spend hours on her phone.'

'So, to cut a long story short, she didn't tell you anything substantial.'

'No, but there was one thing of interest.'

'And what was that?'

'She said that sometimes the girl would make her own bed.'

Montalbano gave him a puzzled look.

'That doesn't seem like such big news to me.'

'Mrs Vullo said that most of the time she herself would make the bed, but on certain mornings she would find it already made.'

'I got that already. So what? Maybe every so often the girl felt like doing some housework.'

Fazio continued, unruffled.

'And this always happened whenever Strangio was away on business and spent the night out. See my point?'

That changed the whole picture.

'I certainly do. Now the whole thing is clear. On the nights when Strangio didn't sleep at home, she would "entertain", let's say, without any fear of unpleasant surprises from her boyfriend. And to prevent the housekeeper from noticing that the bed had been slept in by two people instead of one, she would have it all nicely made up by the time the lady arrived.'

'So it would seem.'

The inspector remained pensive. Then, looking Fazio in the eye, he said:

'We absolutely have to find out who it was that used to go and see her when Strangio was away.'

'Of course,' said Fazio. 'But how? It was only by chance, you know, that I met the housekeeper and found these things out. Otherwise, we'd be completely in the dark. And Strangio's house, except for the big apartment building next to it, is rather isolated. It's unlikely I'll find

123

anyone who can say to me that on certain nights he saw such-and-such a car parked outside the gate until dawn.'

'But we should try anyway, using her as our starting point.'

'Meaning?'

'Fazio, what do we know about this girl? Hardly anything at all. We know she was studying architecture, that her parents don't live in Vigàta, and that she slept till ten in the morning. Don't you think it would be a good idea to find out more? To go into the house, search through photos, papers? And while you're at it, you could have a look at his things too . . . Find out, for example, whether the girl had any female friends, somebody she saw often . . .'

'Chief, the seals have gone up on the house, you know.'

'And I'm not telling you to do a repeat of the supermarket. This time go and get proper authorization from Tommaseo.'

✢

'Catarella? Listen carefully. I want you to search the Rome telephone directory for the number of the main office of Ugotti—'

'Yeah, Chief, I got it.'

'You got what?'

'I'm asposta fine yiz the nummer o' the main office.'

'Yes, but the main office of what?'

'Ya din't tell me the name o' the company, y'only said

to look for the nummer o' the main office, an' then y'ast if I got it, an' I said, "Yeah, I got it." '

The misunderstanding became clear to Montalbano. 'No, Cat, I didn't ask you if you got it. The name of the company I need the number for is *Ugotti*.'

'Now I got it, Chief. Sorry 'bout the quiquivacation. Then whaddo I do?'

'When you get the number, dial it, and when they answer, put the call through to me.'

'Straightaways, Chief.'

Five minutes went by, and the telephone rang.

'Ugotti Computers. Can I help you?' said a crabby, high-pitched female voice with a Roman accent.

'This is Inspector Montalbano, police. I'd like to speak with somebody in management.'

'What about, may I ask?'

'About yesterday's meeting of regional representatives.'

'I'll put you through to Quagliotti. Just a moment, please.'

The moment – with a background of sacred music by Bach, whose connection with computers was entirely un-clear – lasted so long that Montalbano had enough time to review the times tables for 7, 8, and 9.

'Quagliotti here. What can I do for you, Inspector? I should forewarn you, however, that we're not allowed to divulge confidential information over the telephone. It's company policy. It would therefore be best if you—'

'I don't need any confidential information. I just want

to know at what time the meeting of your regional repre-sentatives was held yesterday.'

'From ten a.m. to one p.m.,' the other began, speaking very fast, 'lunch break from one to two, afternoon session from two to five.'

'A final question and I'll let you go. Was Giovanni Strangio at the afternoon session?'

'He signed back in at two o'clock. Whether he left later on, I can't say . . .'

Montalbano thanked him and hung up.

*

All things considered, this wasn't necessarily a solid alibi.

If it happened to come out in the post-mortem that Mariangela was murdered in the late afternoon, Strangio would still have had time to catch a plane in Rome and drive from Punta Raisi airport to Vigàta, snuff out the girl, drive back to Punta Raisi, spend the night in Rome, and head back to Vigàta the following morning.

To confirm this hypothesis, however, one would need to check the flight timetable, and Montalbano had never known how to read any kind of transportation timetable at all – trains, ferries, buses, and especially flights, since those timetables also included information on connections for other cities.

But there was a solution.

'Cat, I want you to call the central police office of

Punta Raisi and ask for the chief inspector. Then put the call through to me.'

'Straightaways, Chief.'

And it really was straightaways.

'Inspector Montalbano? The chief inspector is out at the moment. I'm Sergeant De Felice. You can ask me whatever it is you need to know.'

Montalbano explained the problem to him. 'Could you hold the line?' asked the sergeant.

He came back barely three minutes later.

'OK, I've got the timetable here in front of me, and I can confirm that what you said to me is possible. Here, let me give you the details.'

'I'm sorry, De Felice, but timetables only confuse me. It's enough for me to know that my hypothesis is plausible.'

'Of course it is, Inspector.'

*

He needed another confirmation, however. He rang the Institute for Forensic Medicine.

'Montalbano here.'

'You want to talk to Dr Pasquano?' the attendant asked.

Who else, if not? One of the dead people lying around the morgue?

'Listen, do you know whether the doctor has performed the post-mortem on that girl who was knifed to death?'

'He just finished. Shall I put him on?'

'No, I'd rather speak with him in person.'

'Well, you'd better get here quickly, because he's anxious to go home early today.'

On his way out, the inspector said to Catarella:

'I'll be back in about an hour. If Augello or Fazio come looking for me, I'll be with Dr Pasquano.'

＊

On the way to Montelusa, everything happened.

Two HGVs proceeding side by side for a stretch, preventing anyone from passing them; a minor collision between two cars; and a broken-down bus.

Which caused him to lose a great deal of time before getting to the institute.

He had barely pulled up in the car park when out of the corner of his eye he saw the car right next to him take off like a rocket with a loud screech of the tyres.

As he looked on in curiosity, he saw a hand emerge from the driver's side window and wave bye-bye. It was that bastard Pasquano fleeing so he wouldn't have to talk to him.

He started his car back up and gave chase.

He managed to pass Pasquano's car before it reached the exit gate and to swerve in front, blocking him.

Then, just like a US highway patrolman about to issue a ticket, he got out of his car slowly – regretting only that he wasn't wearing gloves like them so that he could peel them off coolly – and went and bent down at Pasquano's window.

'Licence and registration,' he said.

'I'll give them to you only on the condition that you stick them you-know-where,' Pasquano said angrily. 'What is this? Is an honest man no longer free to go home after a hard day's work? What did I ever do in life to deserve you as my punishment? When the hell are you going to make up your mind and finally retire? Can't you see you're nothing but an old wreck who's falling apart?'

'OK, now that you've got it out of your system,' said the inspector, 'what can you tell me about the girl?'

'What, you think I didn't know that was why you were here? All right, I'll tell you all in one breath so you won't keep on at me. Listen closely, because I'm not going to repeat it. Ready? Forty-seven knife wounds, if you can call them that, of which the first, to the jugular, was fatal.'

'But then—'

'Don't interrupt me or I won't say another word, even if you torture me. The other forty-six served only to vent the killer's rage and were concentrated particularly around the vagina and breasts. Is that clear so far? Don't talk, don't say yes or no; just shake your head or nod. Yes? Then I can go on. The killing must have taken place between five and seven p.m., eight at the latest. I'm sorry for Dr Tommaseo, who will be deeply disappointed, but, despite appearances, the girl was *not*, I repeat, *not* raped. Nor are there any traces of consensual relations. And with that, I wish you the best.'

'Wait a second, please!' said Montalbano, grabbing the edge of the window as Pasquano started the car again.

'Were there any signs of a struggle?'

Pasquano looked at him with pity.

'How could there have been any kind of struggle if I just told you that the first stab cut her jugular?! Can't you see that you're already completely senile? The girl went into the study and was immediately killed.'

'But why did she go into the study naked?'

'How the hell should I know? That's your job to find out.'

'What kind of knife did he use?'

'It wasn't really a knife, but something very sharp and thin. Like a razor or a box cutter, something like that.'

'Have Forensics recovered the weapon?'

'Can't you see you're really not right in the head? If Forensics had found the weapon, I would have told you precisely what was used to kill the girl. Can I go now?'

'Of course. Thanks.'

Montalbano went and moved his car.

Pasquano passed slowly in front of him, then stuck his head out the window.

'Oh, I almost forgot. She was pregnant.'

'How far along?' Montalbano shouted.

'Two months,' Pasquano replied.

Then he accelerated.

*

Now it was late. Before driving back to Marinella, he dropped in at headquarters to see if there was any news.

Not only was there no news, but there was no one there at all except Catarella.

'How far along are you with Borsellino's computer?'

'Jess finishin' up now, Chief.'

'What's inside it?

'The kapewter's got tree icones isside it, one fer corrisponnences, which'd be the litters 'e wrote to diff'rint companies consoinin' the stuff the foresaid was asposta send to the supermarket, y' know, the ordnances . . .'

'Purchase orders.'

'Whativver ya wanna call 'em. An' insomuch as the supermarket riceived 'em more or less inna mount the foresaid supermarket ast fer, annat—'

'OK, I get the picture. What's in the other two?'

'Well, Chief, one of 'em's got the calculations of each day's preceeds . . .'

'Proceeds, Cat.'

'Whativver. Ann'iss is follered by the wickly preceeds, an' then the manthly preceeds, an' then—'

'I get the picture, Cat. What about the third one?'

'Inna toid icone 'ere's the wickly clarence odda moichandise, the clarence—'

'OK, that's enough. Is there anything else?'

'Yeah, I still gotta look at tree more files.'

'All right, I'll be seeing you. I'm going home.'

*

In the entranceway he ran into Augello, who was coming in.

'Can you hang around for another five minutes?' asked Mimì. 'I need to talk to you.'

He seemed clearly agitated.

'Sure,' said the inspector, turning on his heel and heading back to his office.

'I have to tell you what I learned entirely by chance from Fazio, a small detail concerning Borsellino.'

'And what's that?'

'That he didn't commit suicide but was strangled and then made to look as if he'd hanged himself.'

'Didn't I tell you?' asked Montalbano, sincerely surprised.

'No, you didn't. Whereas I'm the first person you should have told.'

'I apologize, I just didn't think of it.'

'Apologies aren't enough.'

'Do you want me to kneel down, too? Are you really so offended?'

'Yes I am. I told you how upset I was over what that idiot journalist said when he accused us of driving Borsellino to suicide, and it would have been a relief for me to find out that he'd been murdered.'

There was something about Augello's attitude that Montalbano didn't like.

'Well, now that you know, you can sleep easy and be happy.'

'Don't try to be funny, this really isn't the time for it. I want you to say it publicly.'

'Say what publicly?'

'That Borsellino was murdered. That way I can sue that journalist.'

'And lose.'

'Why?'

'Because, you see, nowhere has it been said that Borsellino was murdered.'

Mimì became flustered.

'But how did you find out? Fazio told me that Pasquano told you.'

'That's true. He did tell me, but he didn't put it in writing. In his report, that is. He didn't want to put it in writing because, he said, the explanations for the bruises on Borsellino's arms could be given a different interpretation by the defence.'

'It's not Pasquano's business to worry about what the defence might say.'

'Well, he did anyway.'

'But why?'

'Because the Mafia scares everyone, especially when it has ties as powerful as in this case. But I'll make you a deal.'

'I'm listening.'

'I don't want to handle the Strangio case; I'm in a rather delicate position. As soon as he can see me, I'm going to ask the commissioner to turn it over to you.'

TEN

On his way out he again passed Catarella, who was still busy working on Borsellino's computer.

A thought flashed through his brain like a lightning bolt.

'Cat, get me the command office of the customs police of Montelusa and put the call through to my office, would you?'

He went and sat back down at his desk, and the phone rang.

'This is Inspector Montalbano of Vigàta Police. I'd like to speak with Marshal Laganà.'

'Who did you say, please?'

The receptionist seemed a little flustered.

'Laganà.'

'Hold the line, please.'

He could hear him muttering to someone.

'I'm sorry, Inspector. I'm new here. Marshal Laganà retired about a year ago.'

He felt his heart sink. But there was still hope.

'Do you by any chance have a telephone number for him?'

'Wait just a minute and I'll find out.'

After a brief spell, the inspector got the bad news.

'I'm sorry, Inspector, but nobody here has—'

'Thanks anyway.'

*

So how was he ever going to track down the marshal? He remembered that Laganà had once told him he was originally from Fiacca and that he'd inherited a house there from his father . . . It was possible that upon retiring he'd returned to the town of his birth. The inspector rang Catarella and called him into his office. It was better to tell him in person what he wanted him to do.

'At yer command, Chief.'

'Listen carefully, Cat. I want you to call the central police station in Fiacca and find out if they know if there's a former customs marshal named Laganà living there in town. Repeat the name.'

'Lacanna.'

'There's no "canna", for Christ's sake! Laganà. Repeat.'

'Laghianà.'

'Remove the i.'

'I just did.'

'Say it.'

'Laganà.'

'Good. Now don't forget it. If their answer is yes, ask them to give you the phone number, dial it, and then put the call through to me. Got that?'

'Absolutely, Chief.'

But he didn't move.

'Well?'

'Chief, c'n I say som'hn'?'

'Say it.'

'Wouldja 'llow me, isstead o' callin' a Fiacca police an' doin' everyting all roundaboutlike, to take a shortcut?'

There was a shortcut?

'How?'

'I'll jess 'ave a look inna Fiacca phone book t' see if Laganà's in it.'

Montalbano felt humiliated.

'OK, do it.'

It was true that the phone book is usually the last thing that comes to mind when you're looking for someone, but sincerely, this was too much.

Dr Pasquano was right. His advancing age was making him fall apart.

To dispel his agitation, he went over to the window and lit a cigarette. Then the telephone rang.

'I foun' it, Chief!'

'Are you sure?'

'Crass my 'eart, Chief! Iss rilly him! The ix-marshal!'

'Thanks, Cat. Put him on . . . Marshal Laganà? Remember me? This is Inspector Montalbano.'

'How could I ever forget you? What a nice surprise! What a pleasure to hear from you! How are you?'

Better not answer the question. At that moment, owing to this telephone-book business, he felt like shit.

'And you?'

'So so. I had to take an early retirement because of my heart . . .'

'I'm really sorry to hear it.'

'You caught me at home purely by chance, you know. I was on my way out.'

'Oh, really? Where are you going?'

'To Ragusa, with my wife. We're going to visit our grandchildren.'

'How many do you have?'

'Two. A boy and a girl. Did you need something, Inspector? I'm no longer in the service, but maybe I can give you the name of a colleague of mine who—'

'Actually, Marshal, if you've got five minutes, we may be able to resolve the whole thing over the phone.'

'All right, then, what is it?'

Montalbano told him about Borsellino's two computers.

'So,' said Laganà, 'they managed to get their hands on the computer the manager kept at home but not on the one he kept at the supermarket, is that right?'

'Yes, that's right.'

'And you want to know why they wanted both computers?'

'Exactly.'

'There's only one possible explanation. To prevent any-one in the police from getting the idea to compare the two computers.'

'I don't understand.'

'I'll explain. You said the supermarket computer contains among other things the records of the proceeds and the quantity of merchandise sold each day. I'm sure that if you show these files to a colleague of mine, he'll tell you that it's all in order – that the proceeds and sales tally perfectly with each other.'

'But if it's all in order, then why . . . I'm sorry, but I still don't understand.'

'You will in just a minute. If by chance you'd managed to get your hands on the other computer, the one that was in his home, you'd have been able to see for yourself that the figures for the proceeds and the respective sales on a given day were different from the ones registered on the supermarket computer.'

'I get it!' the inspector said finally. 'The figures registered on the home computer were the real figures, while the ones on the office computer were false. They took in more money and sold more goods than what they showed on the, so to speak, "official" computer, the one in the manager's office. But this is all destined to remain purely groundless conjecture because they've now made it impossible ever to compare the two computers.'

'See? You had no trouble understanding. Listen, will you make me a promise?'

'Whatever you like.'

'If you happen to find the other computer, will you let that colleague of mine have a look at it? Wait just a second and I'll get you his number. His name is Sclafani. If my hypothesis is correct, it'll teach those supermarket people a good lesson.'

*

On his way out, he stopped in front of Catarella.

'It's not so urgent about that computer any more.'

'But I'm jess finishin', Chief,' said Catarella, disappointed.

'I didn't say we don't need it any more. I just wanted to let you know you can take your time.'

At that moment Augello walked by, head down, and muttered: 'Goodbye.'

And he headed towards the car park. Montalbano followed him and stopped beside him.

'Still angry?'

'I'll get over it.'

'Mimì, when we spoke in my office, I didn't tell you that the fact that I don't want people knowing about Pasquano's suspicion was because it's a whole lot better for us that way.'

'In what sense?'

'It's important that the killers think that we still believe that Borsellino committed suicide.'

'Do you expect them to make some kind of false move, thinking they're in the clear?'

'Not really, but it's always possible. No, it's better for us because that way, we can work with a murder in mind while they still think we're working on a suicide. Is that clear?'

'Good luck,' said Augello, getting in his car.

'Same to you,' said the inspector in turn. And he turned to open the door to his own car, which was parked next to Mimi's.

'Chief, wait!'

It was Catarella, arriving on the run.

'What the hell is it now?' the inspector asked in irritation.

'Iss 'at 'ere's the lawyer Ne'er-Do-Well onna phone 'oo says 'e's gotta talk t'yiz rilly oigently an' poissonally in poisson. Wha' shou' I tell 'im? Are ya 'ere or not?'

Was it Destiny itself that wouldn't let him go home that evening?

'Go and tell him I'm here.'

Catarella dashed off, whereas the inspector took things easy, lit a cigarette, strolled about the car park while smoking it, then went inside. He found Catarella frozen, with the receiver in hand.

'Count to ten and then put the call through.'

He went back into his office, sat down, and the telephone rang.

'What can I do for you, sir?'

'I'm sorry to bother you at this hour; the switchboard operator said you were on your way home.'

'Don't worry about it. What can I do for you?'

'It's about my client, Strangio.'

'Is there a problem?'

'More than one, unfortunately. You see, after my client gave his deposition to Prosecutor Tommaseo, for which I was not, unfortunately, present, everything has inexplicably come to a halt.'

Montalbano was waiting for a third, conclusive 'unfortunately', but unfortunately it never came.

'Inexplicably? I don't understand, sir. Among other things I don't believe Prosecutor Tommaseo has taken any restrictive measures concerning your client.'

'Well, it depends on how you define "restrictive". If by "restrictive" you mean detention or arrest, then no, that hasn't happened. That would take the cake! My client has an iron-clad alibi!'

Tissue paper would better describe your client's alibi! thought Montalbano.

But he said nothing, asking only:

'So where are these problems?'

'The problems lie in the fact that the prosecutor has strictly forbidden my client to leave Vigàta and has put seals up on his house and garage.'

'But as a lawyer you must know that this is routine procedure.'

'Fine. You, however, are forgetting, as did Prosecutor Tommaseo, that my client is a representative of a Roman firm and therefore needs to be able to move about freely and continuously throughout Sicily. And on top of everything else, he can't even use his car, which is now blocked in his garage.'

'I understand. But I don't see what I—'

'You could at least summon him to the police station to allow him to better explain his situation. That might, at least, shorten his ordeal a little and—'

'Counsellor, it is not up to me but to Prosecutor Tommaseo to interrogate him. He's the one you should be soliciting. Is that clear?'

'Quite,' said the lawyer. 'Good evening.'

Now he could finally go home.

*

In the fridge Adelina had left him a large plate of seafood salad, while in the oven he found some *involtini* of swordfish.

He laid the table on the veranda. It was a gorgeous evening. It took him an hour and a half to dispatch all the food.

He cleared the table, went back out on the veranda with whisky and cigarettes, and started thinking.

What could Duello's phone call mean?

Were they really so stupid as to want him to interrogate Strangio, even without his lawyer present? And without Tommaseo present?

It was known to one and all that the inspector had often and willingly done that sort of thing, not giving a flying fuck about protocol and rules, but this time was different. In this case sudden brainstorms and personal initiatives might severely compromise the investigation.

No, he would play by the rules, down to the last comma.

His thoughts turned to the question of the computers. If luck had smiled on him and Fazio the night before and they'd got their hands on both computers, at this moment the customs police might be able to move against the Honourable Mongibello and the board of directors of the company that owned the supermarket. But that's not the way it had gone – unfortunately, as Nero Duello, Esq., might say. Their night-time search of Borsellino's house and office had been for naught and . . .

He froze.

He had the distinct impression that the entire digestive apparatus in his belly had come to a sudden stop.

He poured himself half a glass of whisky and downed it in a single gulp. Sweat began pouring out of him. How could he have forgotten so completely about it?

This was happening too often lately.

What more proof did he need to convince himself that he was getting too old for his profession?

He remembered perfectly well that he'd taken that sort of tape recorder that Fazio had removed from the breast pocket of Borsellino's jacket and put it in his own jacket pocket.

Afterwards, when he got back home, he'd taken off his detergent-dusted clothes and put them with the clothes to be washed.

So the question now was: had Adelina noticed the recorder in his pocket and removed it before taking the suit to the dry cleaners?

And if the answer was yes, where could she have put it?

He got up and started searching all over the house, throwing everything into disarray. After half an hour of this, he gave up.

He'd once had a similar lapse of memory involving a horseshoe and had nearly lost his life over it. But a horseshoe is one thing, and a recorder is another.

If the dry cleaners had stuck the jacket into the machine without noticing the recorder, goodbye recording!

The only hope was to ring Adelina. He looked at his watch. Eleven o'clock. She'd probably already gone to bed. Well too bad.

'Goo' God, Isspector! Wha' happen? I's aslip!'

'I'm sorry, Adelì, but it's really important.'

'Wha' is it?'

'Did you notice whether there was anything in the breast pocket of the jacket you took to get cleaned?'

'Why, was there somethin'?'

'Yes.'

'I dinna notice 'cause you normally dona keep nothin' in tha' pocket.'

This was true.

'Listen, do you have a number for the cleaners?'

'No, sir.'

'When did they say you could come and get the suit?'

'Day afta tomorra.'

There might still be a ray of hope.

'It must be closed at this hour, right?'

'Yessir. Bu' wait. I jess got a idea. If iss a somethin' sirrious—'

'It's very serious, Adelì.'

'Then I give a you th' address o' the cleaners.'

'But you just said they're closed!'

'Bu' the owner, Mr Anselmo, live a right uppastairs fro' the shop. Th' address is Piazza Libertà, nummer eight. Iss a righta besides the cinema.'

*

He put his clothes back on, left for Vigàta, and, since there was hardly anybody else on the road, ventured to drive at sixty kilometres an hour instead of the legal fifty.

He arrived, stopped, and got out. Next to the cleaners' shop there was a door without an intercom, but only a doorbell and the name Anselmo.

Before ringing, he took two steps back and looked up. Light was filtering out from the balcony upstairs.

He rang. Almost at once the door opened onto the balcony and a man of about fifty, with a moustache and wearing a vest and pyjama bottoms, came out.

The square below was well lit, and Mr Anselmo immediately recognized Montalbano.

'Inspector! What is it?'

'Sorry to disturb you, Mr Anselmo, but I need you to open your shop for me.'

'Sure, straight away.'

There must have been an internal staircase. Moments later the front door of the shop opened.

'Come on in. What can I do for you?'

'Mr Anselmo, a suit of mine was brought to you and—'

'It's already been cleaned. We'll iron it tomorrow.'

Montalbano lost all hope.

'The fact is that in the breast pocket of the jacket there was—'

'Inspector, everything that's brought to us is carefully searched before we put it in the machine. Come over here.'

He went behind the large counter that cut the room in two, and opened a drawer. Inside there were spectacles, fountain pens, driver's licences, ID cards, mobiles . . .

'That's it there,' the inspector said with relief, pointing to the recorder.

He felt like kissing Mr Anselmo on the forehead.

*

As usual, as he was unlocking his front door, he heard the phone ringing. And of course it stopped as soon as his hand was poised over the receiver.

Since tomorrow he was going to put on the same suit he had on now, he left the recorder in the breast pocket of the jacket when he undressed.

He didn't feel sleepy, so he turned on the TV. The purse-lipped face of Pippo Ragonese appeared on the screen.

And so we ask ourselves: whatever happened to the once lightning-quick Inspector Montalbano? The inspector seems to have swung to the opposite extreme. Nowadays he takes things too easy. He hasn't taken a step forward in the investigation of the supermarket burglary that led to the suicide of the shop's manager, Guido Borsellino, which he helped provoke. And as for the horrendous murder of Mariangela Carlesimo, the architecture student, a crime that has shaken the public, and not only in Vigàta, there's no movement whatsoever. We know that the girl's boyfriend, Giovanni Strangio, was ordered not to leave Vigàta. But, since then, nothing. Poor Mr Strangio is left hanging, prevented from——

He turned it off.

Bravo, Ragonese! How many masters did he serve, anyway? The Honourable Mongibello in Parliament and the president of the province both? And they call this journalism? Ragonese only said what he was told to say. They must pay him well.

He then remembered that just a few days earlier, somebody from a private TV station, who wasn't afraid to speak out against the Mafia, had been accused of operating as a journalist without being registered with the Union of Journalists.

So, the inspector thought, *nowadays, in order to fight the Mafia you need the authorization of the Mafia itself.*

They're trawling the net away from the fish!

He went and sat on the veranda to wait for his agitation to pass. But not five minutes later the telephone rang.

ELEVEN

It was Livia.

'How come you're never home when I call?'

'But I'm home right now!'

'No, I mean when I tried earlier.'

'Livia, can I ask you a question?'

'Go ahead.'

'How come you always call me when I'm not home?'

'Well, aren't you good at flipping the pancake! I would never want to fall into your clutches!'

'You've fallen into them many times over. There must be something you like about it.'

'I wasn't referring to that. I meant as someone suspected of a crime.'

'Livia, you know almost everything there is to know about me.'

'Almost? What don't I know about you?'

'Well, for one thing, the way I conduct an interrogation.

To say I flip the pancake and turn things around offends me. I'm extremely fair and above board.'

It was a lie. How many traps had he laid over his career? An infinity.

'I'll pretend to believe that,' said Livia. Then she asked:

'Are you working on the case of that poor girl who was slashed to death with a knife?'

'How did you find that out?'

'It was on the TV news, and I also saw it in the newspaper.'

'Yeah, I'm working on it.'

'Well, be careful.'

'About what?'

'Don't immediately suspect the boyfriend. It's the fashion these days. The moment a girl is killed, they immediately lock up the boyfriend.'

'I don't follow fashion and you know it,' he said, piqued. Then he realized how to get back at her.

'But tell me something, I'm curious. Did you by any chance get a call from a lawyer named Nero Duello?'

'No. Who's he?'

'The boyfriend's lawyer.'

'What are you talking about?'

'I just thought you maybe let him corrupt you into trying to persuade me that the boyfriend is innocent.'

'Idiot,' Livia said in disgust.

And she hung up.

He went to bed. Having got that off his chest, he could fall asleep.

*

The first thing he did as soon as he walked into the station was to stop at Catarella's post, dig out the mini-recorder, and show it to him.

'Cat, what's this, in your opinion?'

Catarella didn't hesitate for a second.

'Chief, 'at'd be a didgytel recorder.'

'Meaning?'

'Meanin' iss a mottified impy tree.'

'And what's a modified impy tree?'

'Iss a mottified impy tree, Chief.'

Better take another tack. Otherwise they would spend the whole morning with him always asking the same question and getting the same answer.

'And what's it used for?'

'Fer many tings, Chief. F'r example, iss a recorder you c'n stick in yer kapewter an'—'

'But do you necessarily have to listen to it on the computer or can you also print out what's on it on your printer?'

'Assolutely, Chief.'

'OK then, I want you to listen to what's on it and print me a copy.'

'The whole ting?'

'The whole thing. How much time is it gonna take?'

'Chief, I got no ways o' knowin'.'

'Why not?'

''Cause it all dipinns on wha' the impy tree's got onnit. One impy tree c'n fit the whole Divine Comity, the whole civil code an' the whole penile code, the hisstry o' the uni-voice, the gaspel, the Bible, an' alla songs o' Di Caprio . . .'

'Di Caprio sings?'

''E sure does, Chief! 'E's been singin' an' singin' fer years! C'mon, ya mean ya don' remimber the one about a voice, a guitar, an'—'

'But you mean Peppino di Capri!'

'In't that what I said? Din't I say Di Caprio?'

Better let it slide.

'Is Fazio here?'

'Nah, Chief.'

＊

Fazio straggled in around eleven.

'The whole morning gone! Tommaseo was in a meeting and couldn't see me. But I decided to wait outside the door, and when he came out to go to the loo, I said I absolutely needed authorization to go into Strangio's house.'

'Did he give it to you?'

'He did, but only orally. He didn't have time to write it down, but he promised me he'd get it to me by this afternoon.'

＊

Fazio went out and the telephone rang.

'Ah, Chief! 'At'd be a jinnelman onna line 'oo calls hisself Lopollo an' says 'e wants a talk t'yiz poissonally in poisson immidiately.'

'What's he want?'

''E din't say, Chief. Bu' when 'e talks ya can't unnerstand.'

'Is he a foreigner?'

'Nossir.'

'So how come you can't understand him?'

''E gots the stubbers.'

The stubbers? The stutters, maybe?

With Catarella, it was always best not to venture too many requests for explanation.

'OK, put him on . . . Hello? Montalbano here. What can I do for you, Mr Lopollo?'

'Lee . . . opo-pò . . . ldo-do . . . tha . . . t's . . . my . . . n-name.'

A moment's distraction and he was already repeating the idiocies Catarella had told him!

'I beg your pardon, Mr Leopoldo. What can I do for you?'

'I . . . I . . . I . . . f-fou . . . nd . . . a . . . d-dead . . . b-b-body.'

'Where?'

'In th-the . . . c-coun . . . try . . . Bo . . . bo . . . rru . . . so . . . d-dist . . . trict . . .'

'And where, exactly?'

'In . . . in . . . th . . . the . . . g . . . gr . . . een . . . h . . . house . . . on th . . . the . . . l . . . le . . . ft . . .'

This was getting painful.

'W . . . we . . . we'll . . . b . . . be . . . r . . . right over,' Montalbano replied.

It was hopeless. Whenever he came into contact with a stutterer, he was immediately infected.

He went into Fazio's office.

'What's up?' asked Fazio.

'Someone by the name of Leopoldo just called. He says there's a dead body in a green house in the Borruso district. Want to bet it's Tumminello?'

'No, because I agree with you.'

'Do you know where Borruso is?'

'Did the guy who called stutter?'

'Yes.'

'Then I know who he is. Filippo Leopoldo. And I also know where his country house is.'

'Is it far?'

'At the ends of the earth.'

'Call Gallo and let's go.'

'Gallo's out with Inspector Augello.'

'Then you and I will go in my car, but you drive.'

*

One got to the Borruso district by way of a track in really bad shape, all holes and mounds.

For the first half-hour the vegetation had grown sparse

and more sparse, and now there was only scorched earth around them, dotted with a few clumps of yellow, wild grass, dead for lack of water.

Every so often, little mountains of white stone looking like piles of bones formed dwarf pyramids, the domains of vipers and hares.

The motion of the car had Montalbano crashing into Fazio one minute and the passenger's side door the next, and at one point the seat belt, which didn't work well, started trying to strangle him. 'How long till we get there?'

'It's just past the next bend.'

Past the bend they saw not only the green house, but also a man walking in front of it.

'That's Leopoldo,' said Fazio.

'Do me a favour,' said Montalbano. '*You* talk to him.'

'Why?'

'My voice is a little hoarse today.'

This was a lie, of course, but how could he ever talk to Leopoldo if he himself started stuttering?

'G-good af-ft . . . ternoon,' Leopoldo greeted them as they got out of the car.

Montalbano returned the greeting with a vague hand gesture.

The green house was made up of two cube-shaped rooms, one on top of the other, and a third cube off to the right-hand side.

The inspector started looking all around the desolate landscape, wondering what mysterious reasons a man might have for building a house in such a godforsaken place. Unless, of course, he was a hermit.

'Over here, Chief,' said Fazio, heading for the third cube, which was a stable with no animals and no door.

He and Fazio went in, while Leopoldo went into the house.

The corpse was curled up on its side, on a bit of straw, as though sleeping. Except for the blood that stained the straw.

It wouldn't be easy to identify him. It was hot, and one could smell that the poor bastard had been dead for a few days already. On top of that, the bullet's exit wound had destroyed his face.

'I think it's him,' said Fazio.

He took the photograph the inspector had given him from his pocket.

'Have a look for yourself,' he continued.

Overcoming his nausea, the inspector crouched down and spent a long time studying what remained of the man's face. Then he stood up.

'I think it's him too, but I'm not sure. They clearly had him kneel down and then fired a shot into the base of the skull. The Mafia's signature. Let's go outside.'

Despite the fact that there was no door, the air in there was unbreathable.

'Did Leopoldo tell you how he found the body?'

'Yes. He'd been wanting to have a new door installed on the stable after he'd used the old one as firewood, since it was already broken up, and so he came in to take measurements.'

They went outside and breathed deep the clean country air.

'Let's do this. You call the three-ring circus: prosecutor, Forensics, and Pasquano. Then ring Gallo, and if he's already back at the station, tell him to come and pick me up. There's nothing for me to do here.'

While Fazio was phoning, Leopoldo came out of his house and walked up to him. He told him something, and Fazio acted as interpreter.

'Leopoldo says that since it's lunchtime, we're welcome to join him at the table. He says he's made rabbit cacciatore and nobody in the world makes it as well as he does. I declined the offer, but if you want . . .'

How long was it since he'd last eaten rabbit cacciatore?

The dish wasn't part of Enzo's repertoire, and Adelina never cooked game.

An irresistible desire came over him.

Leopoldo spurred him on.

'It . . . it's . . . v-ve . . . ry . . . c-cl-ean . . . i-in . . . h-here.'

'I-I . . . n-nev . . . ver . . . d-doubt . . . ed . . . it . . . f-fo . . . for a . . . a . . . m-min . . . ute.'

Leopoldo at first furrowed his brow, thinking the inspector was mocking him, but then, seeing the confused expression on Montalbano's face, he became convinced he was a stutterer just like him.

'S . . . so, wh-wha . . . d-dya s . . . say?'

'I . . . I . . . I . . . ac-cept . . . , th-tha . . . nk . . . y-you.'

As Leopoldo went into the house, Montalbano instructed Fazio:

'Iii . . . if . . . an . . . y . . . of th . . . ose guys . . . c-comes w-when . . . I'm . . . in . . . side, don't te . . . ll . . . an-any . . . one . . . th-that I'm . . . h-here. If th-they ask . . . , t-tell them . . . I . . . I . . . w-went b-back t-to . . . th-the sta . . . tion.'

Fazio looked perplexed. 'I didn't understand a thing, Chief. You feel OK?'

Montalbano took a piece of paper out of his jacket pocket and started writing:

When the others arrive, don't tell them I'm here. Don't call Gallo to come and pick me up.

He got Fazio to read it, then put it back in his pocket and followed Leopoldo into the house.

✳

The meal featured not only an outstanding rabbit cacciatore, but also a dish of spaghetti in tomato sauce, an aged pecorino cheese, some homemade salami, and a nice hearty wine, all of which made the inspector blissfully groggy.

Fazio called Leopoldo to come and give his deposition to Tommaseo.

Montalbano kept on eating.

Leopoldo, moreover, was a perfect tablemate. Since he

had trouble speaking, he ate in silence. He and Montalbano communicated with their eyes. Some two hours later, Fazio came in.

'They've all left. Forensics noticed the victim had his wallet on him and looked in it. His ID card confirmed that he was, in fact, Tumminello.'

He looked at the inspector's plate.

'Any of that left for me?'

And so, to keep Fazio company, Montalbano ate a second helping of rabbit cacciatore.

✻

The road back was a real *via crucis*.

With each jolt, the rabbit jumped up into Montalbano's throat, as if the animal had returned to life and wanted to race back to the pyramid of rocks from which it had carelessly emerged one day only to get shot by Leopoldo.

At about the halfway point Fazio received a call from an agitated Catarella, who said that Mr C'mishner needed to talk immoigently and straightawayslike with Inspector Montalbano.

'What should I tell 'im?'

It wasn't a good moment to talk to the c'mishner, what with the rabbit about to jump out of his mouth.

'Tell him I've gone missing.'

✻

By the grace of God, they finally got back to town.

'Where do you want me to drop you off?'

'By the harbour.'

Before getting out of the car, he asked Fazio:

'When are you going to see Mrs Tumminello?'

'Right now.'

His stomach began to feel a little less heavy after he walked out to the end of the jetty and back twice.

But before returning to the station, he realized he needed to drink a strong double espresso.

*

'Ahh, Chief! Ahh, Chief, Chief!' Catarella wailed, seeing him enter. 'The c'mish—'

'Yeah, I know. Fazio told me.'

Catarella goggled at the inspector.

'So it wadn't true you was done missin'! Man, I'm so glad! Thank the Loord! I's rilly scared!'

'Why?'

'I dunno. Jess the idea of it.'

'Of what?'

'Done missin'.'

'It's "gone missing", Cat.'

'An' wha'd I say? Done missin', no?'

Better let it slide again.

'Listen, how did the commissioner seem to you?'

'Chief, I din't see 'im poissonally in poisson! I only 'oid 'is verse!'

'OK, did it seem hoarse to you?'

'Nah, it juss soun'ed strange.'

'How?'

''S like 'e was a li'l sleepy.'

Was it possible he was still under the effect of the four tranquillizers?

'Get him on the line for me right away.'

'Yessir. But I gotta tell yiz sum'm. I prinnit out every-tin' 'at was onna kapewter.'

'Good! Keep it all in your drawer. An' how's it going with the impy tree?'

'I'm jess startin' on it now. Wan' me t'call the c'mishner?'

'Yeah, call him now.'

*

'At your command, sir! Montalbano here.'

'Ah, yes, hello. What are you calling about?'

A li'l sleepy? Mr C'mishner didn't seem right in the head.

'Mr Commissioner, it was you who called me earlier this afternoon, when I was—'

'Ah, yes. I called you because Dr Lattes told me you urgently needed to talk to me.'

'That's correct, sir.'

'If you want to come now . . .'

'I'll be there in half an hour. Thank you.'

He really didn't sound like the usual Bonetti-Alderighi.

He was completely changed. There was an unprecedented politeness in his tone of voice.

*

Waiting for him in the commissioner's anteroom was Dr Lattes.

'He's on the telephone. Just be patient for a couple of minutes.'

'How are things?'

He was referring to the commissioner, but Lattes misunderstood.

'I'm quite well, with thanks to the Lord. And you?'

'Likewise, with thanks to the same. And how is *he*?'

Lattes seemed a little embarrassed.

'I don't know what to tell you. He's undergone a sort of transformation.'

For better or worse? he wanted to ask, but said nothing. Lattes went up to the commissioner's door, opened it with caution, as if there was a killer on the other side ready to shoot, stuck his head inside, pulled it back out, and turned to Montalbano.

'You can go in.'

Montalbano entered and Lattes closed the door behind him.

Mr C'mishner Bonetti-Alderighi, viewed from the outside, was back to his old self, well groomed and flawless in appearance.

He was sitting as he usually did, straight-backed with

arms resting on the desktop, head leaning slightly back so that his chin was thrust forward, his eyes fixed on his interlocutor.

Except that now the gaze of those eyes was directed not at Montalbano, but to the right of him, where the window was.

'Please sit down.'

Normally he let him remain standing. When Montalbano would sit down, it was always on his own initiative, not upon invitation by the commissioner.

Before he could open his mouth, Bonetti-Alderighi said:

'First of all, I'd like to apologize.'

Never had he heard the commissioner apologize to anyone. He remained open-mouthed, unable to say anything.

'I apologize for the truly ignoble scene I subjected you to the other day. I really wasn't myself, believe me. And I beg you please to forget all about it.'

This new Bonetti-Alderighi intrigued him.

'I've already forgotten it, Mr Commissioner.'

Bonetti-Alderighi turned his gaze from right to left, that is, towards the wall on which hung a tapestry representing a scene from the Sicilian Vespers.

'Thank you. Now, tell me.'

TWELVE

Montalbano was about to open his mouth, but the commissioner stopped him, raising one hand but looking all the while at the tip of a ballpoint pen he was holding in the other.

'I'm sorry, but it seems essential first to make a few things clear. There's no need to remind you that the two cases you have on your hands – I'm referring to the supermarket burglary that led to the manager's suicide, and the murder of the girlfriend of the provincial president's son – will both inevitably be met with political obstructions and reprisals. We've already had the first warning shots from the Honourable Mongibello. Now, I'm well aware that you often neglect to keep me informed of the full scope of your investigations. That you, in short – as you Sicilians like to say – sing me only half the Mass. I'm sure you have your reasons for this, and this is not the time to discuss it. But on this occasion, I'm asking you, for once, to sing me the whole Mass. In your own interest and mine, dear Montalbano. We're in the same boat: do you realize that? And therefore we must row in tandem to steer us away from a whirlpool that could prove fatal to us both. Have I made myself clear? Now you can go ahead and talk.'

He stopped studying the tip of the ballpoint pen and started staring at the fine chandelier hanging from the ceiling.

He'd been extremely clear – not in what he'd said, but in what he hadn't done. He hadn't been able even once, during his speech, to look Montalbano straight in the eye.

And to think that one day he'd confided to him that he always looked at the people he spoke to, because he was able to divine, just by observing their eyes, what they were about to say to him. So why had he avoided doing so this time?

'Well, in keeping with your request,' Montalbano began, 'I should tell you straight away that Borsellino was murdered.'

The commissioner gave a little start in his chair, but kept on staring at the chandelier. Montalbano realized he'd hit the mark. Now he had two options before him: either tell him everything, or sing him the usual half Mass. On the spur of the moment he decided to tell him everything, starting with what Pasquano had told him. If he made a mistake, he would try to correct it.

'It was Dr Pasquano . . .' he began, going on to fill him in on the details.

He told only one lie along the way – which was that

they'd had the prosecutor's authorization for their night-time incursion into the supermarket and Borsellino's home. At any rate the commissioner would never bother to check.

'Unfortunately we have no proof of anything,' Bonetti-Alderighi said by way of conclusion, staring at his left hand.

'So far. But tomorrow morning you'll receive a report on another crime closely connected to the supermarket burglary. It concerns a nightwatchman who had the bad luck to be passing in front of the supermarket when he shouldn't have.'

'Tell me about it,' said the commissioner, eyeing the priceless inkwell he kept on his desk, a present from the Prefecture.

'But you still don't know who killed him,' he added, now staring at his right hand. 'And when you do find out, whoever is behind it all will try to destroy us.'

He sighed, picking up a letter opener and studying its handle.

'And unfortunately I think they'll succeed.'

Another sigh. He turned the letter opener around and started examining the tip.

'And the further we get in the investigation, the more danger we'll be in.'

'Do you want us to stop? Or to start going round in circles, at least?' the inspector asked him.

But not even a question like that could get Bonetti-Alderighi to look at him. So Montalbano decided to force his hand. But how far could he push things? Should he risk it or not? If he didn't, he would never manage to get a clear confirmation of the idea he'd formed of the commissioner's real intentions. So he risked it. He started laughing.

'Do you find the situation amusing?' The commissioner asked the question while eyeing a button on his jacket.

'No, no, on the contrary. But I just remembered something I read once in a novel . . . The story takes place in France. It's about a police inspector who, while investigating a burglary at the home of a daughter of a senior minister, discovers that it's the father himself who ordered the burglary. Not for the jewellery – that was stolen just for cover – but for a rather compromising letter from the minister which the girl was using to blackmail him. As soon as the minister realizes the inspector is on the right track, he threatens to ruin his career. And so the inspector charges a petty thief with the crime and—'

'Excuse me,' the commissioner interrupted him, eyes fixed on the window. 'I assume the thief defended himself?'

'They don't give him the chance. They kill him in a shoot-out.'

'Ah!' said Bonetti-Alderighi, eyes on the chandelier.

There was a long pause.

'Do you still have a copy of this novel?'

'I think so.'

'If you find it, could I borrow it?'

'Of course.'

'Now tell me about the murder of the girl,' the commissioner resumed.

And Montalbano told him at great length about his doubts and the impropriety of his conducting that investigation. Wouldn't it be better, he concluded, if the case were turned over to Inspector Augello?

'It makes no difference whether it's you or Augello,' said the commissioner, staring at a stain on the wooden desktop. 'Everybody knows how much influence you have on your deputy.' He shook his head. 'No, the investigation should remain in your hands. Turning it over to someone else would look like an admission of guilt before the fact. Just carry on and proceed with that sense of fairness and honesty that has always distinguished your work.'

But hadn't Mr C'mishner said a while back that the Vigàta Police were a gang of Mafiosi with Montalbano as the boss?

The commissioner stood up. Montalbano likewise.

'I'd like you to give priority to the investigation of the girl's murder. That way, at least, we won't expose ourselves to malevolent conjectures. And keep me informed on everything,' he emphasized, staring at the lapels of the inspector's jacket.

He held out his hand, and the inspector shook it.

'Never fear, Mr Commissioner. And thank you for your kind words about me.'

*

It was late. By that hour everyone at the station had gone home. He decided to go straight to Marinella.

He hadn't realized that more than two hours had gone by in the commissioner's office, with him doing most of the talking. He'd told him everything, revealing even his conjectures and hypotheses. Bonetti-Alderighi had asked him for complete frankness, and he'd got it.

'We're in the same boat,' he'd said.

Except – and this was something Montalbano had understood from the commissioner's behaviour barely two minutes into their meeting – that Bonetti-Alderighi was ready to push him out of the boat at the first opportunity and let him fall among the sharks circling it.

The man was capable of anything to save himself. The way he'd jumped at the bait of the French novel, which Montalbano had invented on the spot, was proof enough of this. He wanted to borrow the novel to see whether the situation was the same as in the supermarket case!

So now the inspector had to watch his back even with Bonetti-Alderighi.

But having understood what the commissioner had in mind was already a big deal. Because he was sure at this point of having won his superior's self-interested trust. He could therefore tell him whatever he liked and he would swallow it whole.

✻

The first thing he did when he got home was to call Augello on his mobile.

'What did the commissioner have to say?' Mimì asked at once.

'He firmly rejected my request to have the girl's murder investigation turned over to you. He wants me to do it. And maybe it's better for you this way.'

'What do you mean, it's better for me?' Mimì asked grumpily.

'I'll explain tomorrow. I rang you to tell you that as soon as you get to work tomorrow you must summon Strangio and his lawyer to the station for five o'clock.'

He hung up and realized he wasn't hungry. He hadn't digested his double helping of rabbit cacciatore very well.

But he also didn't feel like sitting there going over what the commissioner had said.

He opened the French windows and was greeted by a cool wind that lifted his spirits.

Sitting down in the armchair, he turned on the TV and watched *Once Upon a Time in America* again.

Then Livia called.

'Can you give me half an hour of your time, or are you already half-asleep?' he asked her.

'I can give you even more than half an hour. What do you want to tell me?'

'It's a long story.'

It was always best to have one's hunches confirmed by feminine intuition.

He told her everything: the supermarket burglary, the faked suicide, the commissioner's initial terrified reaction, the murder of the girl, his own doubts, and his last meeting with Bonetti-Alderighi.

'So, what do you think?' he asked her when he'd finished.

'In my opinion Bonetti-Alderighi has given you free rein so that if things go wrong, you'll be the one to take the fall. He's coddling you so you'll become the perfect scapegoat,' Livia replied without the slightest hesitation.

'I agree,' said Montalbano.

'What do you think you'll do?'

'I'll just carry on.'

'Wait a second. Why don't you call in sick and come and spend some time with me?'

'Livia, you ought to know me by now. If anything, I find this new situation stimulating . . . More than that, it's fun.'

'Well, good luck,' said Livia.

✻

The first part of the night he spent tossing and turning in bed. At around five o'clock in the morning, he finally fell asleep and slept through till nine, when he was awakened by the sounds of his housekeeper rummaging about in the kitchen.

'Adelì, bring me a coffee, would you?'

'Comin' right up, Isspector.'

Ah, how wonderful, how comforting to drink one's coffee in bed!

The ceiling of the room seemed to take on a heavenly, light-blue hue.

Then he got up, showered, dressed, and went into the kitchen.

'Would you make me another coffee, please?'

'Issa bubblin' uppa righ' now.'

'What are you making for dinner tonight?'

'Mullet an' onions.'

Maybe, all things considered, life wasn't really so bad, he thought, immediately forgetting his recent digestive problems.

*

As he was entering the station, a jubilant Catarella immediately appeared before him.

'Chief, I finished woikin' onna impy tree.'

'Was there a lot of stuff on it?'

'Nah, jess four conversations wit' people from the supermarket an' then 'is talk – 'im bein' the manatcher – wit' Isspecter Augello an' 'enn 'is talk wit' yiz, which'd be you, Chief, talkin' witta manatcher.'

'Holy shit!' the inspector howled, like a wolf.

Catarella froze in terror.

'Wha'd I say, Chief? Wha', did I do som'n' wrong?'

Wrong? Hardly!

'Come here, Cat.'

Catarella took a step forward, cringing as though fearing that Montalbano might beat him.

The inspector gave him a big hug.

'*Bravo! Bravissimo!*'

Catarella wiped away a tear with the sleeve of his jacket.

A tear of happiness.

'Gad! Ya 'ugged me twice in one week!'

'Where did you put the papers with the transcriptions?'

''Ey're on yer desk, Chief.'

Montalbano ran into his office.

Catarella had outdone himself.

In fact, he'd even given a title to each recorded dialogue. 'Talk with Micheli'; 'Talk with the girl Nunzia'; 'Talk with the holeseller Gesumundo' (who must have been a wholesaler, and whose real name must have been Gesmundo); 'Talk with ya-can't-till-who'; and, lastly, 'Talk with Isspector Augello and with Isspector Montalbano'. The inspector immediately started with the last one, which was the only one that really interested him.

As he was reading it, it became more and more clear that Mimì Augello's behaviour had been utterly proper; he hadn't ventured even once to make any sly comments or insinuations on the likely culprit of the burglary, nor was there ever the slightest hint of irony in his words.

Then he came to Mimì's question:

'*Do you have any idea how the burglar got inside, since there are no signs of forced entry at any of the outside entrances?*'

Borsellino's answer was not only arbitrary, but sudden, and screamed:

'*I want my lawyer!*'

'*But, Mr Borsellino, nobody is accusing you of—*'

'*I want my lawyer!*'

'*Mr Borsellino, look—*'

'*Then I want to speak to Inspector Montalbano!*'

'*But the inspector—*'

'*I want to talk to him!*'

'*Go ahead and call him.*'

This was followed by the two phone calls to the police station, after which Borsellino turned to Augello and concluded:

'*I'm warning you I won't say another word until the inspector arrives.*'

'*As you wish.*'

Here Catarella wrote an ingenious caption:

'In the silentness in the room evry so offen you can hear Isspector Augello whissling a toon I tink is by Cillintano but I'm not sure, and the manatcher paicing back and fort in the room and mambling to hisself.'

Then he, Montalbano, comes in.

At the end, the last things recorded were Borsellino's repressed sobs and the words, '*Best of luck.*'

He picked up the receiver.

'Cat, come in here, would you?'

He hadn't yet put the phone down when Catarella was standing at attention, stiff as a pole, in front of him.

'At your command, Chief!'

'Print me out a copy of Augello's and my talk with the manager, and give me back the digital recorder. And don't forget: don't mention a word of any of this to anyone.'

'I'm silent as a grave, Chief,' said Catarella, handing him the MP3 recorder he had in his pocket.

*

The inspector got in his car and headed off for Montelusa.

Pulling up in front of the Free Channel studios, he parked and got out. The secretary beamed a broad smile at him.

'Haven't seen you for a while, Inspector!'

'Hello, gorgeous. Is my friend in?'

'Yes he is, but he's in a meeting. You can go and wait for him in his office, and I'll let him know you're here.'

Montalbano was one of the family at the Free Channel. And the editor in chief, Nicolò Zito, was a true friend. He waited for barely ten minutes before Zito came in. They embraced.

'All well with the family?' the inspector enquired.

'Quite well, thanks. What have you got for me?'

'We could do each other a favour.'

'Tell me about it.'

'Did you know that the Honourable Mongibello wants to institute a parliamentary investigation into Borsellino's suicide?'

'Of course. I also heard what that puppet Ragonese

said. They want to saddle you with the moral responsibility for the suicide, because in their opinion you tortured him psychologically. It's clear what their purpose is: they want to screw you both – you and the commissioner.'

'As usual, you've understood everything.'

'What do the police intend to do?'

'I haven't the slightest idea what the commissioner wants to do; I only know what I want to do.'

'And what's that?'

'Give you this.'

Montalbano took the digital recorder out of his pocket and handed it to him.

'What's on it?'

'Everything that Mimì Augello said to Borsellino before I arrived, and everything we both said to him after I got there.'

Zito jumped out of his chair.

'Really?!'

'Give it a listen and judge for yourself. First there are four conversations between Borsellino and other people, then there's ours.'

Zito stood there for a moment in silence, then spoke.

'You realize that as soon as I broadcast it, the sky will fall. Surely the judge will confiscate the recorder and—'

'Wait. I'm not interested in the recorder itself. For me, it's enough that you make a copy of what's on it and keep it in reserve for me.'

'Sure, I can do that for you. But that's not the point. I

won't ask you how you got your hands on that recording, but if the judge asks me how I got it, what am I going to tell him?'

'You'll give him the classic answer: you received it in an anonymous parcel with no return address.'

'I may still manage to broadcast it on today's one o'clock report.'

*

As soon as he set foot in the station he went to see Augello in his office.

'Did you summon Strangio and his lawyer?'

'Yes, but the lawyer can't come. He told me to carry on just the same. Doesn't that seem strange to you?'

'It certainly does. He wasn't present when his client gave his deposition to Tommaseo, either.'

'So, can you explain to me why it's better for me not to handle this case?'

'Because you're already risking a great deal by continuing to handle the supermarket case.'

'What do you mean?'

'Mimì, do you remember that I said we were going to have to fight on four fronts?'

'Of course.'

'Well, I was wrong. It's five fronts.'

And he told him about his talk with the commissioner and the conclusion he'd reached.

When he'd finished, Mimì was dismayed, confused, disgusted.

'Now let's go into the conference room,' Montalbano said after looking at his watch.

'To do what?'

'Watch TV.'

The television had been put in six months earlier. An order had been issued that all the police commissariats must have one.

Mimì turned it on and tuned in to the Free Channel. The logo of the news report vanished and Zito's face appeared.

We inform our viewers that straight after our news report we will broadcast a major scoop concerning the suicide of the former super-market manager from Vigàta, Guido Borsellino. As our viewers already know, the Honourable Giulio Mongibello of the majority party has notified the Montelusa commissioner of police that he intends to request a parliamentary investigation of this suicide, which he maintains was provoked by the less than orthodox methods of Inspector Salvo Montal-bano of the Vigàta Police. More specifically, the Honourable Mongibello claimed that Inspector Montalbano subjected Mr Borsellino to veritable psychological torture. We are now in a position to reveal what really happened, thanks to an original recording of the conversation that took place between Inspector Domenico Augello and Borsellino, and the con-versation that took place between Chief Inspector Montalbano and Borsellino. We will broadcast the recording in its entirety, even though it

*contains a gap of roughly half an hour between the dialogue with Aug-
ello and that with Inspector Montalbano. But first the news.*

A good-looking young woman appeared and said:

Good afternoon. Here are today's major news stories.

THIRTEEN

An image of a building under construction appeared.

In Montereale, two illegally employed immigrant workers have died after falling from scaffolding. The courts have opened an investigation . . .

This was followed by the usual burglaries, the usual arson, the usual landings of boats filled with illegal immigrants, and a few attempted murders. When it was over, Zito's face reappeared.

And now we will broadcast the recording we mentioned at the start of this report. For the hearing impaired, we have provided a transcription that can be read on your screen as the audio recording unfolds.

The half-hour in which nobody spoke, but in which you could hear Mimì whistling and Borsellino pacing back and forth, moving chairs, opening and closing the window, and muttering to himself, turned out to be much more

disturbing than any images. When it was over, Mimì Augello was smiling.

It would be quite difficult now for the Honourable
Mongibello to maintain his claim of psychological torture.

*

The inspector went to Enzo's for lunch.

'I've got a huge appetite today,' he said as soon as he
sat down.

And he was served according to his wishes. Seafood
antipasto, spaghetti with a sauce of clams and mussels (a
serving and a half), grilled calamari and scampi (double
serving), wine, no water, and coffee.

When he came out of the trattoria, he realized that a
walk along the jetty was crucial if he wanted to go on
living.

When he came to the lighthouse, he sat down on the
flat rock and started thinking.

Why had Borsellino carefully recorded his talk first
with Mimì and then with him?

There had to be a reason.

Despite the huge meal, his brain was functioning well,
and after an hour of thinking things over, he was convinced
that Borsellino's intention had almost certainly been, at
first, to have the Cuffaros listen to his conversation with
the police so they could see that he had behaved correctly
and hadn't said a single word too many or too few. But
Mimì's question concerning the lack of signs indicating

forced entry had taken him completely by surprise. Apparently that was news to him as well. It seemed that since, when he got to the supermarket, he would normally enter through the rear door, he hadn't gone to check the main doors through which the public entered, one of which the burglar must have forced. Perhaps he realized at that moment that he'd been set up on purpose and that, given this fact, he was now the prime suspect in the burglary. And so he'd reacted the only way possible: that is, by saying he wanted his lawyer. But the ensuing questions that he, Montalbano, asked him left him with no way out. And his weeping, in the end, had been a sort of half confession.

And thus the recording had become useless to Borsellino.

Worse, actually. There was no mistaking the meaning of his weeping.

So why hadn't he erased it?

Maybe that's exactly why he'd gone back to the supermarket; but the killer hadn't given him time. And if the killer hadn't made off with the recorder, as he'd done with the mobile, it was because he hadn't known it existed. And he hadn't looked in the breast pocket of Borsellino's jacket.

Another thing occurred to the inspector.

Borsellino called the police to report the burglary at eight o'clock in the morning, when the shop opened its doors to the public. But the manager must certainly have come in earlier, if only to unlock the entrance for the employees. Was it possible he hadn't noticed the burglary the moment he went into his office? And, if he had, why didn't he report it at once?

Maybe because he'd talked about it with someone.

There were four conversations on the digital recorder, three of which had taken place the day before, since there hadn't been any time for Borsellino to have had them that morning. So the phone call discussing the burglary might actually be the one that Catarella had qualified as 'Talk with ya-can't-till-who'.

But had it been a talk or a phone call?

He glanced at his watch. A few minutes to three. By now Zito must be back at the Free Channel from lunch. The inspector headed back to the station.

'Hello, Montalbano here. Is Zito in?'

'I'll put him on at once.'

'Did you like the broadcast?' Zito asked as soon as he picked up the phone.

'Yes, a lot. Thanks.'

'Dozens of people have been calling in. They're all on your side and against Ragonese and Mongibello.'

'That's nice to know, but . . .'

'But?'

'I don't think popular will or public opinion has any concrete effect on things any more.'

'So, in your opinion, the press and television serve no purpose? Don't they serve to shape public opinion?'

'Nicolò, the press — that is, the newspapers — are useless. Italy is a country with two million illiterates and thirty per cent of the population that can barely sign their names. Three-quarters of those who buy newspapers read only the headlines, which often — and this is another fine Italian custom — say the opposite of what the articles themselves say. The few remaining people have already formed their own opinions and buy whatever newspaper reflects what they already think.'

'As far as the press is concerned,' said Nicolò after a moment's pause, 'I would agree with you in part, but you must admit that even illiterates watch television!'

'And we can see the results. The three biggest private television stations are the personal property of the head of the majority party, and two of the state television stations are headed by men chosen personally by the head of the majority party. That's how your famous public opinion is formed!'

'But my television station isn't—'

'Your station is one of the few exceptions, and it is a truly independent voice. And so I ask you: how many viewers do you have compared to TeleVigàta? One-tenth? One-twelfth? One-twentieth as many? Italians don't like to hear independent voices. The truth troubles their perennially sleepy brains; they'd rather hear voices that don't make any trouble, that reassure them they are part of the flock.'

'I'm sorry, but then why did you turn to me to—'

'So that whoever needed to understand would understand. Listen, let's talk about more serious matters. Has the judge confiscated the recording?'

'Not yet.'

'Have you managed to make copies of everything?'

'Yes. Of everything that was on the recorder. Even the stuff that didn't concern the burglary.'

'That stuff's precious to me, you know.'

'Not to worry.'

'I'll drop in late tomorrow morning to pick it up.'

'Come whenever you like.'

*

Meanwhile he could read the printout of what Catarella called the 'talk with you-can't-tell-who'. He searched through the papers Catarella had given him, but those pages were not among the papers piled on his desktop. Nor were they in the middle drawer.

'Can I come in?' asked Fazio.

Montalbano abandoned his search. He would resume later.

'Did you find anything at Strangio's house?'

Fazio looked disappointed.

'Strangio's correspondence is all business-related. There are a few private letters but of no importance. There's nothing of any interest in the Carlesimo girl's correspondence, either. It's almost all letters from her parents, who live outside Palermo. And there's a few post-cards from a girl friend who must be close to her; she lives here in Vigàta but wrote to her when she travelled. Can I look at a piece of paper I've got in my pocket?'

'Yes, but you know on what condition.'

'Of course, and I'll respect it.'

He took out a small piece of paper, cast a quick glance at it, and put it away again. 'The friend's name is Amalasunta Gambardella, and she lives at number sixteen, Via Crispi.'

Amalasunta! What was the name of the painter who painted Amalasuntas?

'After we talk to Strangio we'll decide whether we need to call her in or not. Anything else?'

'Yes. The girl's diary. The only time she would write things down was when she had to go to Palermo for classes or to the hairdresser, stuff like that. On the other hand, the telephone section has quite a few numbers that need looking into. I've got the diary in my office. Want to see it?'

'No, you study it.'

'Oh, and I also took the girl's computer and gave it to Catarella.'

'How do you know it belonged to the girl?'

'I turned it on and noticed there was stuff related to architecture.'

'And there wasn't any computer belonging to Strangio in his house?'

'No.'

Catarella appeared in the doorway.

'Chief, 'at young guy, LeStrange, 'd be 'ere fer yer 'ter-
rogation. I set 'im down inna waitin' room.'

'Is he alone?'

'Yessir.'

'Go and see if his lawyer's coming.'

Catarella went over to the window, opened it, and
started looking outside. 'What are you doing?'

'What ya ast me to do: I'm lookin' to see if 'is lawyer's
comin'.'

What was this, some kind of Three Stooges routine?

'No, I meant you should go and ask Strangio!'

'Straightaways, Chief!'

'Fazio, I want this all written up.'

Fazio got up and went out. Catarella reappeared.

''E says as 'ow 'ere's no point in waitin' 'cuzza lawyer's
encaged.'

Fazio returned with the computer that a few years ago
had replaced the old typewriter, and he went and sat on
the small sofa.

'Cat, go and tell Augello to come here right away, and
then bring in the young man.'

Mimì appeared immediately and sat down in one of
the two chairs in front of the desk.

Strangio seemed calm. But he was unshaven, and his
eyes were bloodshot. His hands trembled slightly.

'Please sit down,' said Montalbano, indicating the un-
occupied chair.

Strangio sat down and the telephone rang. The inspector picked up.

'I'm not here for anyone!' he yelled, hanging up.

'Mr Strangio . . .'

The phone rang again.

'Ahh, Chief! Ahh, Chief, Chief!'

It was the commissioner.

'Put the call through to Augello's office,' he said, and then, to those present in the room: 'Sorry, I'll try to get this over with as quickly as possible.'

He raced to Augello's room, where the phone was already ringing as he entered.

'Hello? Montalbano here.'

'I've learned about the Free Channel broadcast of—'

'Yes, Mr Commissioner.'

'I'm very pleased, because it shows unequivocally that you and Augello acted quite correctly. And I think that any accusations against the two of you would at this point be groundless.'

Why did he say 'the two of you' instead of 'us'? Wasn't he himself a member of the police force? Were they no longer in the same boat? This was a mistake unworthy of Bonetti-Alderighi's intelligence.

'I agree with you, sir.'

Was it possible the commissioner had called only to congratulate him?

'Ah, listen, Montalbano. Do you have any idea how that recorder ended up in that journalist's hands?'

Here was the real reason for the phone call.

'No idea at all, Mr Commissioner. When I searched Borsellino's home and office, there was no sign of it.'

'Well, if anything should occur to you . . .'

'I shall dutifully inform you at once.'

Love and kisses, goodbye. He went back to his office.

Clearly, during the time he was out of that room, nobody had said a word. The silence was as thick as a shroud of smoke. 'You, Strangio, when you would go away for work, would you phone your girlfriend Mariangela?'

'Of course.'

'Even when you went to Rome?'

The young man smiled.

'When I went to Rome I would call her several times. Upon arrival, then in the afternoon, and again in the evening.'

'Did you do so also on the—'

'Of course. But my last call to her was around five p.m. that day.'

'Did she say anything unusual to you at that time?'

'She said she had a terrible headache and was going to go to bed early, and she asked me not to call her again in the evening, as I usually did.'

'Did she seem calm?'

'Totally calm. Normal.'

'How did you call her? On your mobile?'

'No, from a public phone.'

'Why?'

'Because I hadn't gone to my hotel yet, and my mobile was out of juice.'

'Then you must have recharged it later, since you declared to Prosecutor Tommaseo that you rang your girl-friend several times on your drive back to Vigàta from Palermo airport.'

'Yes, that's right. I recharged it as soon as I got to the hotel.'

'What's the name of the hotel you stayed in?'

'The Sallustio. If you want the number—'

'No, that's all right, thanks. I don't need it. Now I want you to try and remember what you did after your business meeting.'

'After the meeting? I went out to dinner and—'

'Do you usually dine at five p.m.?'

Strangio smiled again. This time, however, it was a sly little smile that rather irritated the inspector.

'I can see you've done your homework. I went wander-ing around Rome.'

Montalbano had the distinct impression the young man was not telling the truth.

At this point the inspector had an idea. He would bluff, with all due respect to Livia. Before speaking, he performed a bit of theatre, à la Bonetti-Alderighi. He picked up a ballpoint pen, studied the tip with great inter-est, put it back in its place, and then said very seriously:

'Mr Strangio, I find myself compelled to ask you to

rethink the last answer you gave me. Would you like to change it?'

'No. Why would I?'

'Because Inspector Augello, here present, has already called the Sallustio Hotel. As you yourself noticed, we've done our homework concerning your stay in Rome.'

Strangio went as stiff as a salted codfish and didn't open his mouth. Montalbano turned to Augello.

'Tell us what they told you.'

Mimì proved equal to the challenge.

He slowly pulled a piece of paper out of his jacket and pretended to read what was written on it. 'The customer left the hotel in the afternoon, after paying his bill.'

He folded the paper up again and put it back in his pocket.

Strangio fell straight into the trap, clothes and all, that they'd laid for him.

'The fact is that I absolutely do not want . . .' he started with effort, a lot more nervous than before.

'Wait, Mr Strangio. I would like to put on the record my profound regret that your lawyer isn't here, although I'd alerted him as to our meeting beforehand. You can, if you wish, refuse to proceed any further.'

Strangio didn't give it a moment's thought.

'Let's carry on. The sooner we get this over with, the better.'

'Fazio, did you put on the record that I made it clear to Mr Strangio that we could, upon his request, suspend the interrogation? Yes? All right then, we can go on. Mr Strangio, can you tell us what you did after the meeting?'

The young man swallowed twice before opening his mouth.

'I wanted to avoid involving . . . Yes, it's true, I dropped in at the hotel, paid the bill, got them to call me a taxi, and then I went . . . to see a friend, a woman.'

'And what time was it when you got to this friend's place?'

'I dunno . . . around six-thirty.'

'What did you do with her?'

'We . . . talked. And then we had dinner. We ate in. Because . . . I'd told her I was free.'

'Did you sleep there?'

'Yes.'

'And from there you went to the airport the following morning?'

'Yes.'

'Do you look up this friend of yours every time you go to Rome?'

'Yes.'

'So she's a steady lover of yours?'

'Yes.'

Good for Strangio and his Roman mistress!

'Can I smoke?' the young man asked.

'No, not at the moment. How long have you been in a relationship with this woman?'

'About two years, except for a period of interruption that lasted a few months.'

'Was your girlfriend aware of this situation?'

'No.'

'I want this girl's first and last name, address, and telephone number.'

'Couldn't we keep her out of—'

'No, Mr Strangio. You should realize she's your alibi.'

'All right, then, if it can't be avoided . . . Her name is Stella Ambrogini, and she lives on Via Sardegna, number 715. Her phone number is 06 321 7714, and her mobile is 338 55833. She can confirm everything. But . . .'

'What?'

'At the press conference I said I slept at the hotel.'

What was he talking about?

'You held a press conference?!'

'Yes.'

Montalbano started swearing under his breath. He noticed that Fazio and Mimì also seemed stunned.

'Why?'

'They were so insistent!'

'Who?'

'The journalists.'

A question came out of the inspector's mouth before he could hold it back.

'Was your father in agreement with this?'

'My father's not around. He's in Naples and will be back this evening. I haven't told him anything.'

'Where did you hold the press conference?'

'At my dad's house, where I live at present.'

'Was your lawyer there?'

'No.'

Of course not! The guy was never around. If he hadn't actually seen him in person, Montalbano might doubt that he even existed.

'Excuse me, Mr Strangio, but I need to interrupt things for a moment. Fazio, take him to Catarella, who can escort him outside to have a cigarette, then show him into the waiting room. But you come back here.'

Fazio and Strangio went out. 'Well done, Mimì! I can see we haven't lost our feel for team play.'

'Thanks.'

Fazio returned and sat down in Strangio's chair.

'This business of the press conference caught me unawares,' said the inspector. 'What do you two think?'

'He denies it, but it might be a move his father suggested to him,' said Mimì.

'I don't agree,' said Fazio. 'His father normally uses journalists like Ragonese. The kid clearly isn't quite right in the head, and to expose his son like that, without even his lawyer at his side, doesn't seem like the sort of thing a clever man like the provincial president would do.'

'I agree with Fazio,' said the inspector. 'It was a brilliant idea cooked up independently by the kid himself. But the real question is: to what end? There must be a reason.'

'Listen, we'll just have to wait and watch the press conference this evening, then we can discuss it,' Augello
concluded.

'The main new development is that Strangio seems to
have a solid alibi,' said Montalbano. 'Fazio, go into your
office and call this woman. See whether she's willing to
confirm everything in front of a judge. I'm going to go and
have a cigarette.'

'But Strangio's already in the courtyard,' said Mimì.

'So I'll smoke in the toilet.'

FOURTEEN

When Montalbano returned, Fazio and Mimì were in his office, chatting.

'Did you talk to her?'

'Yes, sir. Apparently Strangio had already informed her. She knew about the murder. She's ready to confirm everything in court.'

'Confirming it in court doesn't mean anything,' said Mimì. 'People lie under oath all the time.'

'And for that reason, we'll carry on,' said Montalbano. Then, turning to Fazio:

'Go and get Strangio.'

*

'Were you in love with your girlfriend?'

The young man hesitated for a moment.

'I was very fond of her.'

He said it the same way somebody might say he had been very close to his dog, who had just died. He seemed to realize this, and so felt compelled to explain.

'After we'd been living together for about two months, Mariangela and I became . . . well, good friends. Even though we did happen, now and then, or even often, to sleep together. We both realized we'd made a mistake; there was no more rapture, no more passion. Affection, yes. A lot. It was like . . . a wind that suddenly drops. That's how it was.'

'Did the two of you talk about this new situation?'

'Of course. At great length, even. We decided that we should each live our own life.'

'Well, you weren't legally bound to each other: why did you keep living under the same roof?'

'I dunno. Maybe – though this may sound strange – out of laziness. I think . . .'

'Go on.'

'I think – but it's just a guess on my part, mind you – I think that over the last few months, Mariangela, feeling herself emotionally free, may have . . . become interested in someone else.'

'What makes you think that?'

'Well . . . A certain change of mood . . . She . . . yes, she'd started seeming more cheerful again, more . . . But at other times she was also very sad, closed . . .'

'She was two months pregnant,' Montalbano shot out.

Augello and Fazio were even more surprised than Strangio.

'Oh, really? She never told me.'

A pause. Then:

'Who knows whether I was the father . . .'

Neither worried nor pleased. Just mildly curious. 'That period you mentioned, when you broke off relations with your girlfriend in Rome, when was that?'

'During the first two months I was living with Mariangela.'

'Do you have any idea who might be the man Mariangela became "interested" in, as you put it?'

'I haven't the foggiest idea.'

The answer had come too promptly. Maybe he did have an idea, and not a very foggy one at that.

'When, on your return from Palermo airport, you got home and opened the door . . . Speaking of which, was it locked?'

'Of course it was locked. Mariangela, especially when she was alone, was always afraid that—'

'Did you notice any signs of forced entry?'

'No, there weren't any. Or, if there were, I didn't see any.'

'Can you confirm that you came directly here, to the police, after discovering the murder?'

'Yes, I can. I landed at Punta Raisi airport at nine, was here in Vigàta by ten-thirty, and at eleven I came to the police.'

'Only an hour and a half from the airport to Vigàta?'

'Yes. I'm a good driver. An hour and a half if there's no traffic, naturally.'

The telephone rang.

'Ah, Chief! Proxicutter Gommaseo jess called an' since I said you was encaged wit' Stranger, 'e said to tell yiz, meanin' you, to tella foresaid 'atta Proxicutter Gommaseo's waitin' f'r 'im, not f'r yiz, 'oo'd be you, butta foresaid Stranger, t'marra mornin' a' nine-toity in 'is affice in Montelusa a' nine-toity tamarra mornin'.'

'Prosecutor Tommaseo will be waiting for you tomorrow morning, though it's a Sunday, at nine-thirty, at the courthouse of Montelusa,' Montalbano communicated to the young man.

Then he said:

'I think that's enough for today.'

'There's something that doesn't make sense to me,' Strangio said unexpectedly.

'What's that?'

'When I saw Mariangela from the hallway, she was naked and lying on the desk in the study. Did you find any of her clothes in the room?'

'No.'

'That's strange.'

'Why?'

'Normally, before going to bed at night, she would shower and then go around the house in a white bathrobe made of terrycloth. Did you find it?'

'It wasn't in the study.'

'There's another thing ... Prosecutor Tommaseo wanted me to put my car in the garage, and then had seals put up on the garage. I forgot my computer in the car, and without it I can't even work. I'd like to have it back. Is that possible?'

'You can ask Prosecutor Tommaseo tomorrow. And listen: make sure that your lawyer is also present tomorrow morning. Mimì, please show the gentleman out.'

They said goodbye, and Augello and Strangio left.

'I want you to summon Mariangela's close friend for tomorrow morning,' the inspector said to Fazio, 'even though it's Sunday. After what Strangio told us, we absolutely need to talk to her.'

*

When Fazio had also left, the inspector resumed looking for the pages with the transcriptions. He couldn't find them anywhere. And so he concluded that he'd probably taken them home to Marinella.

By now it was late. He rang Tommaseo, hoping to keep things short.

'Montalbano? Are you coming too tomorrow morning?'

'Actually, I have—'

'Doesn't matter. Did you pressure him well? I've worked out how Strangio killed her, you know.'

'Oh, really? Tell me.'

'It all revolves around flight timetables. Listen closely. So, Strangio flies out of Rome on the—'

'I had the same idea, sir, so I informed myself. What you are suggesting would be possible only if—'

'See? You yourself came to the same conclusion. And Dr Pasquano has even supplied the motive! She was pregnant! Strangio discovers that Mariangela is pregnant, becomes suspicious, since he's almost certain that he's not the father, and then, in a jealous rage, he decides to kill her. So he catches a flight out of Rome—'

'We've already said that.'

'Ah, right.'

'The problem is, Strangio has a solid alibi.'

'What alibi?'

'He spent the night in Rome with his mistress. And the girl is ready to testify in court.'

'But the testimony of a call girl is basically worthless!'

Montalbano was stumped.

'Do you know her?'

'No. I don't even know her name, you haven't told me.'

'So how can you say—'

'I just know by intuition!'

'Look—'

'Trust me, Montalbano, I'm right on this. Come on: you've got in your hands a wonder of nature, a gem, a sheer delight, a fragrant flower, a jewel of a—'

'I'm sorry, but who are you referring to?'

'To Mariangela, of course! I'm looking at her photos as we speak. So you've got in your hands an angel and you go with a woman of sin like that call girl, who for a handful of cash is ready to bear false witness?'

Could Tommaseo be falling hopelessly in love with the dead Mariangela? If so, Strangio, whether guilty or innocent, was going to be put through a meat grinder. Better clear things up immediately.

'I'm sorry, Mr Tommaseo, but I think you're making a big error of judgement.'

'Oh, really?'

'Yes. I don't agree with your focusing the investigation only on Strangio.'

'Listen, Inspector. Who is directing this investigation?'

'You, sir. But I repeat: I don't agree. There's still a whole array of—'

'Well, if you don't agree, you know what will happen? I'll be forced to talk about this with the commissioner.'

'Do as you see fit.'

*

He'd gone this far, he might as well go all the way. Instead of taking the road to Marinella, he turned onto a parallel road, Via Pirandello, the one that led to Strangio's house. He'd had Fazio give him the keys. He parked outside the gate, which had been left open, and got out of the car. There wasn't anyone on the street. He walked down the little lane, up to the front door, removed the seals, opened the door, went inside, and closed the door behind him. He turned on the light and went upstairs.

The smell of blood was still strong in the study. He looked at the desk on which they'd found Mariangela sprawled out in an obscene pose. As if the killer had murdered her as they were about to make love.

He went out of the study and looked back in from the hallway. Strangio had been telling the truth: from there you could see everything. There was no need for him to enter the room to realize what had happened.

He went back in. On the large desk were some files with the name Ugotti on them, books, architectural designs, city maps, urban-planning manuals, large sheets of transparent paper, drawing paper, pencils of many different colours, erasers, highlighters, T-squares . . . all drenched in blood.

The white bathrobe was not in the study.

He looked for it all over the house but didn't find it. Perhaps the killer had taken it away with him, maybe putting it in an ordinary plastic bag.

But why did Strangio place so much importance on this bathrobe?

The inspector went out again, locked up, and put the seals back in place. Then he went down the little street that led behind the house, which was called Via Brancati.

Here was the garage, with seals on it. He removed them, raised the rolling door, and a little slip of paper fluttered in the air and onto the floor. Curious, he turned on the garage light in order to see better, then bent down and picked it up. It was a small flier with the words *SLEEP EASY Security Institution.*

Apparently the nightwatchman, when he passed at night, would slip a flier between the garage door and the wall to show that he'd done his job. When one raised the door, the slip of paper fell to the ground. The inspector wanted to do a test. He lowered the garage door, stuck the paper in, then raised it again. The paper fell out. He picked it up again and started staring at it, then realized that there were another three on the ground that must have been there for a few days already. He picked these up, folded them, and put them in his pocket with the other one. There was something that didn't add up, but he couldn't work out what. He went into the garage.

Inside was Strangio's BMW. A computer was visible on the back seat. At the opposite end of the garage was another rolling door exactly the same as the one through which he'd entered. He raised this one too. Here, too, they'd put up seals. He was now in the garden.

It was a convenient setup. One arrived by car on Via Brancati, put it in the garage, and then entered the house through the garden, without having to backtrack on foot. Just as one could enter through the gate with the car and then put it in the garage by opening the inside garage door.

He locked everything up again, went out onto the street, and put the seals back in place.

Happening to look up, he noticed, on a fourth-floor balcony of the apartment building next door, a woman looking out at him. She was definitely the same woman he'd seen sunning herself the first time he'd come to the house. Was the woman out on her balcony day and night?

He went back to his car and drove home.

❈

He looked all over the house for those transcriptions but didn't find them. The only possible explanation was that someone had taken the pages away when they'd come to pick up the documents he'd signed. He would ask Catarella about it in the morning.

As usual he laid the table on the veranda, then went to get the dish of mullet and onions that Adelina had prepared. A sheer delight. But he didn't savour them fully as they deserved, since he had something on his mind that prevented him.

He finished, cleared the table, replaced the dishes and cutlery with whisky and cigarettes, then went back inside to get the leaflets, spread them out on the table, sat down, and put them in chronological order.

There were four of them, and they went from the fifth of the month to the eighth.

It seemed all in order. He was wasting his time. On the other hand . . .

He grabbed the bottle and was about to open it when, at that exact moment, a light gust of wind carried away the leaflets. With both his hands occupied, he was unable to prevent them from flying away. Cursing the saints, he started chasing them down. Two came to rest on the floor of the veranda itself, the third ended up on the sand not far away, while the fourth disappeared. Muttering ever new variations of curses, he ran into the house, grabbed a small pocket lamp, and went back out. It took him ten minutes to find the other leaflet. At last he had it in his hand.

Meanwhile, however, he'd realized why the whole thing

hadn't added up for him from the start, from the moment he'd entered the garage.

But he needed immediate confirmation; otherwise he wouldn't sleep a wink that night.

He went to the phone, bringing the leaflets with him, and dialled a number.

'Fazio. Sorry, I know it's late, but—'

'What is it, Chief?'

'You were there when Tommaseo sequestered Strangio's car and told him to put it in the garage, weren't you? Tell me how it went.'

'Strangio's car had been left with us. So Gallo and I brought him back to Vigàta, and then Strangio drove it back to his place with us following behind him. But Strangio didn't turn onto Via Brancati; he went in through his front gate, down the driveway that leads to the garage, raised the garage door, and put the car inside. Tommaseo then had seals put on both garage doors.'

'One more thing. Do you remember Strangio saying that when he got home from the airport, he put the car in the garage and then went through the garden to get to the house?'

'Yeah, I remember.'

'And then he said that, after discovering the body, he took his car back out to come to us?'

'Yeah, that's right.'

'Thanks. Good night.'

To pre-empt the danger of the wind, he lined up the

leaflets on the dining-room table and then sat down in front of them.

So poor Mariangela was murdered the evening of the seventh. Strangio, who had already left – as proved by the leaflet marked the seventh, which had fallen on the floor of the garage – came back the morning of the following day, the eighth, and, according to his declaration, opened the garage door. As a result, the slip for the eighth should have fallen to the ground.

Whereas in fact it had stayed in place.

Nor could it have fallen when Tommaseo ordered Strangio to put the car in the garage, because he came in through the other door.

The slip for the eighth should no longer have been there, if things had gone the way Strangio said they had.

And if it was still there, this meant that things had not gone the way the young man had said.

So what had actually happened?

What happened was that Strangio, home from the airport, had not gone through the garage, but had parked the BMW outside the gate.

As if he already knew that he would need the car again shortly afterwards to race to the police station. As if he already knew what he would find in the study.

He gathered the slips, stuck them in his pocket, went out on the veranda, and knocked back half a glass of whisky while waiting for Livia to call.

He didn't want to think about anything. Staring at the sea was good enough for him.

*

He woke up at seven-thirty. *Why bother to get up?* he thought. It was Sunday; he could take things a bit easy. He closed his eyes again. Less than ten minutes later the phone rang. He got out of bed to answer. It was Nicolò Zito, sounding upset. 'Half an hour ago I got a phone call at home from a woman with the cleaning service who'd found the front door to the Free Channel studios broken in. I called the commissioner's office and then raced to the scene.'

'What did they steal?'

'Can't you imagine for yourself? There was only one thing on my desk.'

'The digital recorder?'

'Exactly.'

Montalbano felt his heart sink.

'What about the copy?'

'No, luckily I'd brought it home with me. But I wanted to let you know.'

The inspector breathed a big sigh of relief.

'Thanks.'

'But there's one thing I can't understand. Don't they realize it's pointless and stupid on their part? They should also have stolen the tapes of last night's news broadcast. They were right there.'

'Nicolò, it's not like these people are always that smart.'

He hung up. There was no point in going back to bed. He went into the kitchen to make coffee.

Though he hadn't wanted to say so to Zito, the burglars' act made sense. It was clear that they were interested in everything that was on the recorder, not just the part that had been broadcast.

At this point he started thinking about the fact that to cover up a burglary of limited scope – Fazio was right about this – they'd already killed two people and committed another burglary that would certainly make some noise, because it had happened at a television studio. Zito was certain to describe it on the air as an intimidation tactic and ask for solidarity on the part of his professional colleagues.

In short, whoever stole the recorder knew that it would unleash total pandemonium, but they did it just the same the moment they heard that Borsellino had kept a recorder hidden in his office. They must have said to themselves: *Want to bet he also recorded the conversations he had with us before reporting the burglary?*

And they had acted accordingly, wasting no time and not giving a damn about what the papers and TV would say.

*

He showered, shaved, dressed, drank another half-mug of espresso, then the telephone rang again. And this was supposed to be a quiet Sunday morning?

By now it was eight-thirty, and this time it was Fazio who was calling.

'Sorry, Chief, but last light I forgot to tell you that Mariangela's girlfriend is coming into the station at ten o'clock, after she gets out of Mass. I'll be there too.'

'OK.'

'Did you watch Strangio's press conference yesterday, which they broadcast again at midnight?'

'No, I forgot. How'd it go?'

'Strangio said the same things he told us, except that he said he'd slept at the hotel in Rome. And you know what? The most troubling question he had to deal with was put to him by none other than Ragonese.'

'And what was that?'

'Actually, it wasn't really a question. Ragonese pointed out to him, timetable in hand, that in leaving his meeting a little early, he had all the time he needed to catch a plane, come here, kill his girlfriend, and go back to Rome.'

They'd all thought the same thing!

'Strangio,' Fazio continued, 'said only that he didn't kill his girlfriend. But Ragonese's harangue had its effect. I'd been expecting him to defend the kid, whereas he threw down an ace.'

'Thanks, Fazio, I'll see you in a bit.'

And this meant simply that there were two orders from on high: the supermarket burglar must turn out to be Borsellino, and Mariangela's killer must turn out to be Giovanni Strangio.

But how on earth could his father, Michele, the powerful president of the province, let his son be accused in this fashion without reacting?

*

So how was he going to pass the time now? Lolling about the house? No, there was a better way. He went out, got in the car, and headed for Vigàta. But instead of continuing on to the centre of town, when he got to the first houses he turned onto Via Pirandello and pulled up in front of the gate outside Strangio's house. He got out of the car and looked up. The lady on the fourth floor was on her balcony. He went on foot to Via Brancati and came to a stop in front of Strangio's garage. He raised his hand and waved to the lady. She waved back. He cupped his hands around his mouth and said:

'I'd like to talk to you.'

'Fourth floor, apartment sixteen,' the woman said, using the same method.

As he approached the main door, he looked at the names on the intercom system. Apartment sixteen corresponded with the name Concetta Arnone. The door clicked; he pushed it open, went inside, and took the lift. The woman was waiting for him outside her door.

'Please come in, Inspector.'

'How do you know who I am?'

'I've seen you on TV. What, you think I'd let in a total stranger just because he waved to me from the street?'

FIFTEEN

She looked somewhere between sixty-five and seventy years old, was well groomed, didn't wear glasses, had a well-preserved face, with few wrinkles and lively eyes, but she must have had something wrong with her legs, as she couldn't bend them. She sat the inspector down on the sofa in the small living room and then sat herself down beside him.

'My legs are stiff; it's very hard for me to walk,' she began.

In the first fifteen minutes of their talk, Montalbano learned that she'd lost her husband five years earlier, had no children, had a married sister in Fiacca, had her shopping done by a woman neighbour of the kind they don't make any more, had trouble making ends meet with her pension, had nothing to do all day but stand out on the balcony leaning on the railing, since sitting was too uncomfortable, and watched television late into the night . . .

The inspector interrupted the monologue.

'Signora, I need you to tell me whether you were on your balcony on the morning of the eighth, and whether by any chance you saw—'

'The eighth was a Thursday,' said the woman. 'Cannoli day.'

'I don't understand.'

'I have a sweet tooth, Inspector, and on Thursdays I ask my neighbour to buy me a cannolo. One on Thursday, and the other today, which is Sunday.'

'I wanted to ask you whether on the morning of Thursday the eighth, around ten-thirty, you saw Giovanni Strangio, the young man who lives in the house—'

'Of course I know Strangio, and I knew his girlfriend too, poor thing. Yes, I saw him that morning.'

'He told us that when he got back from Palermo, he put his car in the garage and then—'

'No, sir, he did not put it in the garage.'

Montalbano pricked up his ears.

'He didn't?'

'No, sir. He stopped outside the garage – I recognized the car – but he didn't get out. He just stayed there a few minutes and then left. Come with me.'

She got up with effort, and Montalbano followed her.

So he'd been right about the security service's slips of paper!

From the balcony you could see the garage and the entire garden of Strangio's house.

'The young man just sat still inside the car as if thinking things over, then started it up again and drove away. When he got to Via Pirandello, he turned left.'

'Are you sure about that?' Montalbano asked in surprise. If he turned left, this meant that he went directly to the police station. For him to stop in front of the gate and then go and find his girlfriend's dead body, he would have had to turn right.

Therefore Strangio hadn't even felt the need to go into the house. There was no point. He'd already been told what had happened inside. And the only person who could have told him this was the killer himself. A killer whom Strangio didn't want to accuse, as in so doing he would risk being taken for the killer himself.

'. . . and that's why, I repeat, he turned left,' the woman concluded.

Montalbano had missed what she'd just said.

'I'm not doubting you, signora.'

'An' I can see well even in the dark,' she said. 'All I need is the light from that streetlamp there – see it? – and I can see like it's day.'

'I believe you.'

'An' you know what? I want to tell you something with no disrespect to the soul of that poor girl who was killed.'

'Tell me.'

'Let's just say that for the last three months and more, even four, there was a man who came to see her in the evenings when Strangio was away.'

Montalbano held his breath.

'What he would do was this,' the woman continued. 'He would pull up outside the garage, get out of the car, open the door – apparently he had the keys – put the car inside, and then come out the back. I would see him walk through the garden and then disappear round the corner of the house.'

'So he went into the house.'

'Of course, otherwise I'd have seen him coming out the gate.'

'Did you ever have a chance to see his face?'

'Never. I always saw him from behind.'

'But when he came back out of the house to go back to his car—'

'He must have always left very early in the morning. I never saw him come out. I'm always sleeping at that hour. The only thing I can say is that he wasn't a young man, but at least fifty years old. I could tell by the walk.'

'You said these visits occurred when Strangio was away?'

'That's right.'

*

Before going back to the station, he went first to a *pasticceria* and ordered a tray of twelve cannoli.

Catarella had the day off and was replaced by an officer named Sanfilippo.

'Is Fazio here?'

'Yes, sir.'

'Tell him to come to my office.'

As soon as Fazio came in, Montalbano handed him the pastry tray.

'Take this into your office, and after we've finished with the girl, I want you to deliver it to Mrs Concetta Arnone, who lives on the fourth floor of the apartment building on Via Brancati.'

Fazio's eyes sparkled.

'Did she tell you something important?'

'Extremely important. Go and put this tray away and I'll tell you everything.'

But they didn't manage in time, because the moment Fazio sat back down, Sanfilippo came and announced that a woman by the name of Amalasunta Gambardella had just arrived.

✻

The inspector had noticed in the past that the bosom friends of beautiful girls were usually rather plain. And Amalasunta did not break the mould.

Bespectacled and shabbily dressed, she nevertheless had a determined air about her.

'If you hadn't sought me out, I would have come to you myself,' was the first thing she said.

'We summoned you here because Inspector Fazio, when looking through the deceased's correspondence, realized you were her best—'

216

'He's right,' Amalasunta cut him off. 'She used to tell me everything.'

'So you can be a big help to us.'

'I think so too.'

'So let's start at the beginning. When did you first meet Mariangela?'

'We used to be classmates in elementary school and remained friends ever after.'

'So you must know how Mariangela and Giovanni met?'

'Of course. The father introduced her to him.'

Montalbano was momentarily at a loss.

'I'm sorry, but whose father?'

'Giovanni's father, the Honourable Michele Strangio, president of the province.'

Clearly Amalasunta wasn't terribly fond of the Honourable Strangio.

'And how did Giovanni's father know her?'

'He was her teacher at secondary school, at the *liceo scientifico*. Her maths professor. Mariangela was his pupil. When Giovanni and Mariangela met, she was in her third year.'

'I see,' said the inspector.

'No, I don't think you do,' the girl said breezily.

'What do you mean?'

'I mean that four months ago Professor Strangio resumed the relationship he had with Mariangela when she was still in secondary school.'

Montalbano felt as if the chair beneath him were wobbling from a mild tremor in the earth.

'But are you sure about what you're—'

'Shall I go into the details? How and where it happened the first time?'

'And nobody ever found—'

'Do you know Professor Strangio? He's a very good-looking man, a widower, extremely charming, he speaks like a god, he's spellbinding. As soon as he entered politics it became his career.'

'How old is he?'

'Fifty-five, fifty-six. But he looks younger.'

'So nobody at the school ever found out?'

'No. People used to whisper that Strangio went with his girl students, but it was always just rumours, just gossip.'

'Was Mariangela in love with him?'

'Sort of. Just enough, in her own mind, to justify sleeping with him. But when the professor introduced his son to her, Mariangela had the impression that his intention was . . . well, that he wasn't introducing him without some self-interest . . . that he was . . . I don't know how to put this . . . that he was sort of trying to "park" her with Giovanni.'

'Why didn't she rebel?'

'Mariangela had many gifts, on top of her beauty. But she was weak-willed and would let herself be dragged into things.'

'And why did Giovanni accept?'

'Inspector, Giovanni is totally dominated by his father. He does everything the man asks of him, without saying a word. And Mariangela was gorgeous. Boys used to lose their heads over her. And Giovanni has been under the sway of his father ever since childhood. His father has always wanted him to be like a real son to him . . .'

Another mild tremor in the ground.

'Why, is he not the professor's son?'

'No, he was adopted at the age of five. The professor's wife, who died four years after the adoption, couldn't have children. And that was how Giovanni grew up, and it's why he's not really all there. It's his father's fault, because of the way he's always treated him.'

Fazio and Montalbano exchanged a glance. They'd struck gold.

'Listen, I have to ask you a question, and I'd like you to answer with the same frankness you've shown us thus far. Did Mariangela tell you she was pregnant?'

'Yes.'

'Was Giovanni the father?'

'No.'

'Do you know who was?'

'Yes.'

'Can you tell me his name?'

Before answering, Amalasunta heaved a long sigh. 'Inspector, when we entered the university, Mariangela chose architecture and I chose law. And I like it a lot. None of what I've told you so far is of any strictly criminal consequence to anyone. But if I tell you that name, the whole picture changes. On top of that, I don't think that there's any evidence that might prove the guilt of the person I would name. And Mariangela is dead, so no one could ever ask her whether I'm telling the truth or not.'

She would become an excellent lawyer, this Amalasunta; that much was clear.

'Was the father of the child the man who had been going to see her for four months when Giovanni was out of town?'

The girl didn't answer.

'There's an eyewitness,' Montalbano pressed on.

'And he recognized the man?'

'In a certain sense.'

The girl thought this over for a moment.

'I think you're setting me up, and I'm not going to fall for it.'

She was smart, and shrewd. Montalbano didn't comment.

'Did Mariangela have any other lovers?'

'No.'

'Listen, would you also refuse to name this person in front of a judge? Let me explain. You study law, and therefore you should know that your refusal to reveal this person's identity could cost you, and dearly.'

'I know.'

'So you, in full awareness, refuse to give me the killer's name.'

The girl's composure and resolve suddenly vanished.

'But whoever said he was the killer?'

'Come on, you yourself suspect that Mariangela's lover, the same one who got her pregnant, might also be her killer. Since it's only a suspicion, however, you don't want to name him. But, you see, your attitude leads me to think that if this person were just anybody, you would have no problem naming him. The fact that you won't is because you fear the consequences.'

The girl could only hang her head and look at the floor.

'Because we're talking about a very important person,' the inspector continued, 'who could, if he wanted, take revenge on you. I understand you, you know. I'll tell you what. I won't ask you to name him.'

The girl remained in the same position.

'And I won't name him either,' Montalbano continued. 'Though not out of fear. But because I don't have any proof yet. When I do have proof, will you be willing to confirm the name, even in court?'

This time the girl raised her head and looked at him.

'In that case, yes.'

'Thank you for everything. You can go now.'

The inspector stood up and held out his hand to her. The girl shook it. She said goodbye to Fazio and headed for the door but stopped when Montalbano asked:

'Could I start my investigation with the hypothesis that the whole thing began with the rekindling of an old flame?'

The girl turned around.

'Yes,' she said, and then left.

'Did you get all that, Fazio?'

'Of course. What do you think I am, an idiot?'

'Then get moving, even if it's Sunday. Start making phone calls, gathering information, get all of heaven and earth involved. And don't forget the cannoli for Mrs Arnone.'

Fazio had barely left when the outside phone rang. It was Mr C'mishner.

'Ah, good, I was really hoping to find you, Montalbano. I just got a long phone call from Prosecutor Tommaseo, who tells me that you're not in agreement with his line of investigation. Tommaseo leans towards complete culpability, whereas you supposedly have serious doubts. Is that correct?'

He didn't once mention Strangio's name. Was he afraid the phone might be bugged?

'It's not that I have serious doubts, it's just that I took the liberty of suggesting to Tommaseo that we also follow other leads.'

'But are there any?'

'Look, just this morning, but purely by chance, I talked to a lady who told me that she saw a man pay the girl a visit several times, always at night and always when her boyfriend was away. She even saw his face.'

He paused and then fired another lie.

'A tall, good-looking young man of about thirty, driving a two-seater sports car.'

The commissioner remained silent for a moment. He was weighing his options. The arrest of Giovanni Strangio was certain to trigger some enormous political headaches, whereas the arrest of any old killer would cause no trouble at all. On the contrary.

'Listen, Montalbano. Let's do this. I'll assign Rasetti to Tommaseo's investigation, and you continue to follow the lead of the thirty-year-old. I'm giving you verbal authorization, naturally.'

'Naturally. Thank you, Mr Commissioner.'

*

He hung up and went to Fazio's office to search through all the papers he'd signed, which were about to be shipped out, for those pages with the transcriptions of the recordings. At last he found them. He folded them and put them in his jacket pocket.

He went out, got in his car, and went to Enzo's to eat. He really couldn't complain about the morning's catch.

After eating, he took his customary stroll along the jetty and then headed home.

*

He took his clothes off and got into bed.

'I'll just rest for a few minutes,' he said to himself.

Instead he slept till five, when he was woken up by a phone call from Fazio.

'Chief, can I come over with Inspector Augello?'

'Come.'

He had just enough time to have a shower and get dressed before he heard the doorbell.

'I dropped in at the station and ran into Fazio, who told me everything,' said Mimì. 'So I thought it was best if I came too.'

They sat down on the veranda. It was a stunning Sunday afternoon. There were many people lying on the beach enjoying the westering sun.

'Can I get you two anything?'

'Nothing, thanks,' the two replied in chorus.

Then Fazio, without asking permission, pulled a piece of paper out of his pocket. 'There's nothing from the records office,' he reassured Montalbano. And he continued:

'On the morning of the murder, the president of the province had a meeting that lasted until one p.m., went to lunch, had another meeting that lasted until five, and then said he was going home to pack, because he had to leave for Naples to attend another political meeting.'

'We need to check whether—' the inspector began.

'Already taken care of. He took the nine o'clock flight out of Palermo.'

'That would have given him all the time in the world to murder Mariangela,' said Mimì.

Montalbano seemed not to have heard him.

'We need to find out what hotel—'

'Already taken care of.'

Montalbano shot to his feet, leaned against the veranda railing, took three deep breaths, and succeeded in dispelling the agitation that had come over him due to Fazio's use of that phrase. He sat back down.

'He stayed at the Hotel Vulcano,' said Fazio.

If, in response to his next question, Fazio replied again with 'Already taken care of,' the inspector might not be able to control himself any longer. So he asked it in another way.

'And naturally you've informed yourself as to which flight Giovanni took from Rome to Naples to meet his father, who had summoned him there.'

Mimì looked puzzled, whereas Fazio smiled.

'Yes, sir, I have. He didn't take any flight at all, as it turns out. He rented a fast car from Avis, which he left at Fiumicino airport early the next morning. His Roman girlfriend didn't tell the truth.'

'At any rate, he therefore couldn't have come here to kill the girl,' Augello concluded.

'Listen, guys,' said Montalbano. 'To recapitulate, here is how things might have gone. The professor feels his old flame for Mariangela rekindling, and the two resume their former relationship. But the girl gets pregnant and tells her lover. She doesn't want to get rid of the kid; maybe she even insists that the professor marry her. And if he won't, she threatens to create a scandal. On the evening of his departure for Naples, the president goes to see the girl, perhaps to try again and persuade her to abort. They have a violent altercation. The distinguished president loses his head, thinking that a scandal would ruin his political career, and kills her with a box cutter he finds on the desk. He butchers her hatefully. Then he takes off her bathrobe, puts her in an obscene pose to make it look like a crime of passion, picks up the bathrobe, goes out, locks the door to the house, enters the garage through the back door, puts the bathrobe in the boot of his car, and races desperately to the airport after calling Giovanni and making an appointment to meet with him in Naples. When his son arrives at the hotel in Naples, he tells him everything and persuades him to help him. He promises to get him the best defence lawyers. And the kid, who's in no condition to say no to his father, accepts. And you know the rest.'

'Nice reconstruction,' said Augello. 'Even plausible. But I don't understand the stuff about the bathrobe.'

'Let me explain it to you, Mimì. She was wearing it when Strangio started slashing her with the box cutter. Almost certainly, in his frenzy, he cut himself as well. And since he could easily be screwed by an eventual DNA test, he's forced to take the bathrobe away with him.'

'But surely Strangio's suit, shirt, and shoes must also have been covered with blood!' Mimì objected.

'Of course they were. But he changed them in the garage and put on some clean clothes that he had in his suitcase. Don't forget, he'd gone to the girl's house with a packed suitcase.'

'But there's something I don't understand,' Fazio cut in. 'Why did Giovanni mention the bathrobe to us in the first place?'

'Look, Strangio senior left it in the boot of his car when he arrived at the airport. He didn't throw it out of the car on his way there, as he did with the box cutter, because a bloodstained bathrobe, if anyone found it, might attract the attention of the police or carabinieri. And he didn't have time to stop somewhere and bury it. So as soon as he gets to Palermo he asks his son to get rid of it. And the kid takes it out of his father's car and puts it in his own. But he doesn't get rid of it.'

'Why not?' asked Fazio.

'Because, perhaps for the first time in his life, it dawns on him that he's taking too big a risk by obeying his father. That bathrobe, if the worst comes to the worst, could be his salvation. And when he realizes that he's seen neither hide nor hair of all the lawyers promised him by his father, he begins to take cover. *That's* why he told us about the bathrobe.'

He looked at Fazio.

'Shall we bet I'm right?'

'I already told you once: I never bet when I'm sure to lose. Have you got the keys to the garage?'

'Yes, let's go inside and I'll give them to you.'

'Give me also a large plastic bag to put it in.'

*

Montalbano and Augello had a glass of whisky while waiting. It took Fazio about twenty minutes to go to Strangio's and come back.

'It's in my car. What should I do with it?'

'Take it to headquarters and lock it up. And now, while we're at it, let's talk about another story, the supermarket.'

SIXTEEN

'Speaking of which,' said Mimì, 'I wonder who it was that sent that recording to the Free Channel. Maybe . . .'

Fazio stared at his toecaps.

'Nobody sent it: I took it there myself,' said Montalbano.

Augello sat upright in his chair.

'You?! How did you get it?'

'We found it by chance, Fazio and I did, the other night, when we went into the supermarket.'

'And what were you doing there?'

'To tell you the truth, I didn't really know at the time.'

'But why didn't you turn the recorder over to the prosecutor?'

'Mimì, think for a second. First of all, because we entered the supermarket illegally. Second, because the prosecutor would have told us that before deciding what to do with the recorder, he would have to discuss it with the chief procurator, then with the prefect, then with the bishop, then with the American ambassador, and in conclusion he would have informed us that the recording, having no evidentiary value in court, had to be destroyed.' Mimì said nothing. Then Montalbano let his two men know what he'd been thinking: that the recorded discussion that preceded Mimì's arrival might be about the burglary.

'Let's hear it,' said Augello.

'I left the recorder with Zito, but last night the Free Channel offices were broken into and the only thing that was stolen was in fact the recorder . . . However, I'd told Zito to make a copy of the recordings, and this is still in his possession. To make up for it, however, I've got here the transcriptions Catarella made of those recordings for me.'

He went into the house, found the papers, selected the one titled 'Talk with ya-can't-till-who', and went back out on the veranda. Before reading it aloud, the inspector gave it a quick glance. And he immediately understood that it involved not a tête-à-tête conversation, but an exchange over the phone. Borsellino must have held the recorder in such a way that it would also pick up the voice of the man at the other end. Borsellino was the first to speak.

'Hello? This is Guido.'
'I told you not to call me at this number.'
'I'm sorry, but it's an emergency.'
'OK, but be quick about it.'

'*Last night somebody stole the day's proceeds at the supermarket that I—*'
'*Yeah, yeah, go on.*'

Here there was a momentary confusion on Borsellino's part.

'*I'm sorry, but—*'
'*Just talk, for God's sake!*'
'*But how did you know—*'
'*Come on, keep talking!*'
'*I want to know what I should do.*'
'*You're asking me?*'
'*Who should I ask if not you, who are—*'
'*Listen, just do what you think is best.*'
'*Can I call the police?*'
'*Do what you think is best, I said.*'

End of conversation. Montalbano, Augello, and Fazio just sat there, speechless, looking at one another in astonishment.

'Sorry, Chief, but could you reread that for me?' asked Fazio, pulling himself together.

The inspector reread it from the start, stressing practically every syllable. Then he put the sheet of paper down on the table and said:

'Contrary to what he told us, Borsellino did inform someone of the burglary. And the man cut him loose immediately. He didn't give him a helping hand; he just let him drown. But the more serious implication for us is that Borsellino was not in cahoots with the burglar, which is what we'd always thought. On top of this, the man talking to Borsellino already knew about the burglary before the manager called him. Do you two agree?'

'Yes,' said Augello. 'Even if he doesn't say explicitly that he already knows.'

'Borsellino blurts out what he says in surprise, but he's already perfectly aware that the other man knows. And that's probably when he starts to smell a rat.'

'But if he was innocent, why did he start crying in front of us?' asked Fazio.

'Precisely *because* he was innocent. Because he realized that the burglary was a setup by the Cuffaros to back him into a corner. He was desperate, he'd done everything to get himself arrested, which was the only escape route he had left, and we didn't do it. We left him in his killers' hands.'

'But we couldn't very well have imagined . . .' Augello began.

'No, Mimì, there are no justifications. I got the whole thing wrong, all down the line. I should have paid more attention to what you said, Fazio.'

'What did I say?'

'Have you forgotten? You maintained that two murders to cover whoever stole less than twenty thousand euros seemed disproportionate to you. There must be something much bigger behind all this.'

'So what do we do now?' asked Augello.

'Now we must try to think this through with cooler heads,' said Montalbano. 'One thing is certain. The intention of those who put this whole plot together was to make it look as if Borsellino was complicit in the burglary. And that our suspecting him was what drove him to suicide. So they wanted to kill him, but without it looking like a murder. The Mafia, however, normally just kills without making such a production out of it. But here we're looking at some very fine stage direction. If it was the Cuffaros, they've been guided by a much more subtle mind. Whatever the case, the question is: what did Borsellino do or say to merit a death sentence? Fazio, do you know how long he'd been manager of the supermarket?'

'Ever since it opened three years ago.'

'So it must be something that occurred recently. We have to find out what happened.'

'I'll try,' said Fazio.

Mimì got up.

'I have to pick my wife up and take her to the cinema.'

'I'm leaving too,' said Fazio.

'Oh, listen, Fazio. Do you have Michele Strangio's telephone numbers?'

'Not with me here, no. I'll give them to you as soon as I get to the office.'

Fifteen minutes later he had the numbers.

*

He enjoyed the sunset, still seated out on the veranda. And after the sunset, he also enjoyed the evening's first darkness. Then he got in his car and drove off, because, it being Sunday, Adelina hadn't come, and so he had to go out to eat.

He felt like amusing himself, so he went to one of those seaside restaurants in Montereale Marina where they serve an infinity of wonderful antipasti. The whole time he was eating he couldn't stop thinking about Michele Strangio, the illustrious president of the province. Since Strangio junior would never dare tell the truth, the good president felt safe, and would have no problem letting his son go to jail. But would he, Montalbano, be able to remain silent in the face of such a sordid, rotten affair? No. They had to flush out the beast, make him come out into the open.

When he got back home it was past eleven. He undressed, got comfortable in front of the television, channel-surfed until midnight, and then tuned in to TeleVigàta. The chicken-arse face was on duty.

. . . our editorial offices have just received news that Commissioner Bonetti-Alderighi has relieved Inspector Montalbano of the investigation into the murder of Mariangela Carlesimo and turned it over to Inspector Silvio Rasetti. The replacement was made upon the request of Prosecutor Tommaseo, who found himself seriously at odds with Inspector Montalbano over the conduct of the investigation. Apparently the inspector is not entirely convinced of the guilt of Giovanni

Strangio, the prime suspect, who was taken to prison this afternoon on the charge of aggravated murder. We can only applaud both the replacement of Inspector Montalbano as well as the arrest of Strangio, a decision promptly made by Prosecutor Tommaseo, who has shown us how justice must never hesitate, not even for political reasons, when faced with a murder of the kind that . . .

He turned off the TV. He'd already made up his mind. The announcement of Giovanni Strangio's arrest had given him the final push. But he'd known since the afternoon, since the business of the bathrobe, that he would end up taking this course of action. What he had in mind was not, of course, something an honest man would do. But how do you remove shit from the middle of the street without a shovel and bag? You have no choice but to use your hands and get them dirty.

But what he had in mind to do he couldn't do from his home telephone. It was too dangerous. He put his clothes back on, took a clothes peg from the broom cupboard, a big chunk of bread from the kitchen, and, from the first-aid box, a handful of cotton and a roll of gauze bandage. Sticking it all in his jacket pockets, he went out, got into the car, and pulled up at the Bar Marinella, which had a public phone in a booth out of the patrons' sight. The rolling shutter in front was halfway down. He'd been lucky; the bar was about to close. He crouched down and went in.

'Michè, I have to make some phone calls; my home phone doesn't work.'

'You can take your time, Inspector, the bar's closed.'

Just to be discreet, the owner went outside for a breath of air.

The inspector put the clothes peg over his nose and tested his voice, which came out nasal.

He dialled the home of Michele Strangio. The president should be back from Naples already. If not, he would call him on his mobile. A masculine voice, peremptory and irritated, answered after the sixth ring.

'Hello? Who is this?'

'Is this Professor Strangio, Michele Strangio, president of the province?'

'Yes.'

'Could you give me your address?'

Strangio blew up like a powder keg.

'You're calling me at this hour to know my . . . ?! How dare you! Tell me who this is!'

'I want to send you an anonymous letter.'

'Oh, give me a . . . If this is some kind of joke, I'll have you know that—'

'An anonymous letter about a bathrobe stained with your blood and that of Mariangela Carlesimo.'

Strangio said nothing. The explosive revelation must have taken his breath away. Montalbano hung up. He took the clothes peg off his nose, grabbed the chunk of bread, stuck it in his mouth, and redialled the number. This time he spoke in dialect.

'Hello? Who is this?'

Strangio's voice had changed dramatically. It was trembling now.

'Hullo? Dis is a frenn' o' the guy 'at called yiz a few minniss ago. So, whatta we gonna do 'bout dis battrobe?' And he hung up. He went to the counter, spat out the bread, then put the handful of cotton over his mouth, holding it in place with the gauze, which he wrapped around his face.

Tutankhamen's mummy. He redialled the number. Strangio picked up at once.

'For pity's sake, I beg you . . .'

'How much are you willing to pay?'

'Whatever you want, three million, four . . .'

'I didn't mean money, moron, I meant years in prison.' He hung up again. He removed the cotton and gauze and put it all in his pocket.

Stepping out of the bar, he thanked the barman and then drove back home, where he got ready for bed. He was certain he would have an excellent sleep. Just as he was equally certain that Michele Strangio would have a night of hell.

*

At just before nine o'clock the next morning, he was in the office, looking good and feeling fresh and well rested.

'Cat, make me a copy of this, would you?' he said, handing him the sheet of paper with the transcription of Borsellino's telephone conversation with the unknown person. 'But leave out the title you put there, the "talk with you-can't-tell-who". Then find me an envelope addressed to me, but without any inscription or return address.'

Catarella sat there looking mystified.

'I din't unnastan' a ting, Chief.'

It took him ten minutes to explain what he wanted, but then five minutes later he had what he wanted on his desk.

'Get me Hizzoner the C'mishner on the phone.'

The envelope was open, inside it a letter from someone reporting that his wife was cheating on him. Montalbano took the letter out and in its place slipped in the sheet of paper, folded in four, with the transcription of Borsellino's phone conversation. Then he put the envelope in his jacket pocket. The telephone rang.

'Montalbano here, Mr Commissioner. I need to confer with you on a rather urgent matter, good sir.' *Confer* was OK, but *good sir* was perhaps a bit over the top.

'I too need to tell you something. Come at once.'

*

'We won!' the commissioner exclaimed as soon as the inspector walked in.

'In what sense, may I ask?'

'In the sense that just a little while ago the Honourable

Mongibello paid me a visit. On his own initiative. And he immediately apologized. He claimed there'd been a misunderstanding on his part. That he'd been misinformed and will make amends for everything he said about us. And that he will make a sort of public retraction through Pippo Ragonese's news broadcast.'

'So he's not calling for a parliamentary question any more?'

'He assured me there's no longer any need.'

Now came the best part. But he had to use kid gloves. He made a dark face.

'Unfortunately, a new front has opened up with Mongibello,' he said, sounding worried.

The commissioner immediately got more worried than him.

'Oh my God! Are we back to square one?'

'Worse, I think. I've made a very big mistake, Mr Commissioner.'

'Concerning the supermarket investigation?'

'Yes. As you know, I've always thought that Borsellino was killed because he was an accomplice to the robbery. Well, I was wrong.'

'But what evidence do you have to claim—'

'An anonymous letter, sir. It's not really a letter, but the transcription of a telephone exchange between Borsellino and an unknown, maybe somebody with the Cuffaros.'

He took the envelope out of his pocket, took out the

sheet of paper, and handed it to the commissioner, who read it and gave it back.

'As you can see, sir, we can clearly infer that Borsellino knew nothing about the burglary.'

'Do you have any idea who might have sent this to you?'

'The same person who sent the recording to the Free Channel.'

'But how do we know that this is a transcription of an actual conversation?'

'The burglars told us.'

'What burglars?'

'Perhaps you haven't had a chance yet to read the report. On Saturday night, unknown persons broke into the Free Channel studios and stole the very same digital recorder that contained the conversations that were aired. I'm convinced that this phone call, the one transcribed on this piece of paper, occurred shortly before Inspector Augello and I arrived at the supermarket.'

'I suppose you may be right, but without that recorder, we don't have any real proof. But what does Mongibello have to do with any of this?'

It was the only thing that mattered to the commissioner, and Montalbano gave him satisfaction. 'Mr Commissioner, the starting point in this whole affair is the supermarket burglary. The burglar was able to enter by using the key kept by the board of directors of the company that owns the supermarket. Now it just so happens that the managing director and president of this company

— which is entirely a front for the Cuffaros — is the Honourable Mongibello. In my opinion, he's involved up to his neck in this affair.'

Bonetti-Alderighi started swearing under his breath, then stood up, walked once around the room, sat back down, stood up again, walked halfway around the room, then sat back down.

'Stay calm, Montalbano, stay calm,' he said.

'I'm perfectly calm,' said the inspector.

'We need to proceed very delicately with this.'

'With kid gloves? Mine are already on.'

'We must use caution, great caution.'

Montalbano, the phony good soldier, replied:

'I totally agree with you, sir.'

The commissioner was sweating visibly. The telephone rang. Little by little, Bonetti-Alderighi, as he listened, looked more and more like a corpse.

What could they be telling him? Then the commissioner spoke.

'I'm on my way.'

And he hung up. He took out a handkerchief and wiped his forehead.

'The president of the province, Michele Strangio, has shot and killed himself. His housekeeper found him this morning. He left a letter exonerating his son. It was him who killed that young woman.'

Montalbano sat completely still, in a daze. At that

moment, the commissioner, who was staring at him, asked him the most intelligent question of his life.

'You . . . suspected the president, didn't you?'

Montalbano managed to stand up and assume the pose of an offended man.

'Whatever are you saying? If I'd had the slightest suspicion in his regard, I would have done my duty and informed you at once . . . The witness said she'd seen a thirty-year-old . . .'

'I have to go now,' said the commissioner, leaving the room.

Montalbano sat down again. He was unable to walk; his legs had turned into ricotta cheese. He hadn't guessed that his phone calls might lead to this. He'd been falsely accused of driving a man to suicide, yet now that he had, in a way, done just that, no one could ever possibly accuse him of it. But maybe it was better for everyone this way.

*

He pulled up in front of the Free Channel studios, parked, and got out. The secretary did not smile at him this time. She looked worried.

'Mr Zito's not in,' she said. 'Two carabinieri came for him, and he left with them. He asked me to phone Mr Sciabica, his lawyer, and I did.'

'But do you know what he's accused of?'

'Yes. The lawyer called about five minutes ago. The

judge doesn't believe that burglars broke in here. He says Mr Zito faked a burglary so he wouldn't have to turn over the recorder to him.'

'Do you know who the judge is?'

'Yes. Armando La Cava.'

Poor Zito! He couldn't have happened upon a worse judge. La Cava was a Calabrian with a thick Calabrian head – that is, when he got his mind set on something, there was no changing it, not even if Jesus Christ appeared before him in person.

'Please ring me at the station as soon as you have any news.'

*

The news of Michele Strangio's suicide made him not want to go to the office any more. He drove down towards Vigàta, but at a certain point he turned and took the road to the temples. Moments later he found himself walking amidst a group of Japanese tourists photographing everything in sight, even blades of grass. The long stroll whetted his appetite, and since it was the right time, he went to Enzo's. He ate without stuffing himself, but took a stroll out to the lighthouse just the same. When he got back to the station, Augello and Fazio were waiting for him.

'Did you have anything to do with Strangio's suicide?' Mimì asked him right off the bat.

'Me?! What are you thinking? How could I possibly have had anything to do with it?'

Fazio looked at him but said nothing. It was clear he hadn't swallowed it.

'What are we going to do with the bathrobe now?' he asked.

'For now, just keep it here. If Strangio doesn't mention it in the letter he left behind, we'll get rid of it. Shall we pick up where we left off yesterday?'

'Chief, I haven't even been back home to eat,' said Fazio.

'Why, what happened?'

'What happened was that after asking a question I got a half-answer that was worse than a bomb.'

Montalbano and Augello both pricked up their ears. But Fazio was a master of the art of suspense. The inspector decided not to press him, and to let him relish his moment, to make up for the fact that he hadn't eaten.

'And what was that?' asked Augello, less sensitive than Montalbano.

'Two people reluctantly told me something nobody's talking about.'

He paused again and then fired.

'Apparently Borsellino was kidnapped.'

Montalbano's and Augello's jaws dropped.

'Kidnapped?!' they said in chorus, stunned.

Fazio basked in the success he was enjoying.

'Do you know for how long he was kidnapped?' Montalbano asked.

'Four days.'

'A flash kidnapping,' Augello commented.

'Mimì, sometimes you make discoveries that even Einstein could never have come up with!'

'I blush.'

'Was a ransom paid?'

'So they say.'

'Who did they demand the money from?'

'The Cuffaros.'

'The Cuffaros?!'

'Chief, who else were they going to ask? Borsellino had no family and I don't think he had much money either.'

'So what did the Cuffaros do?'

'Apparently they paid a large sum without argument.'

'Naturally, they took care not to report it to us or the carabinieri.'

'Naturally.'

'Does anyone have any theories as to who might have been behind this?'

'At first everyone blamed the Sinagras, but they managed to convince everyone they had nothing to do with it.'

'I wonder how they managed that,' said Mimì.

'Mafiosi always understand one another in a hurry,' said Montalbano. 'And so?'

'And so nobody knows who it was.'

'Maybe some desperadoes who tried to pull off a nasty coup and succeeded,' Mimì ventured.

'Listen, but what did he himself say about what happened?'

SEVENTEEN

'Chief, I'm just telling you the rumours that are going around. One evening he got a phone call summoning him to a board of directors' meeting at nine o'clock the same evening. A supplier was present who later told his friends what happened. He said that Borsellino started swearing because there hadn't been any advance warning and he didn't have his papers in order. Borsellino later said that as he was about to head home late that night, since the meeting had gone on for ever, a car pulled up beside him. Two men got out, grabbed him, and forced him to get into their car, which then sped off. Moments later they shoved a handful of cotton soaked with chloroform over his nose and he passed out.'

'He didn't get a look at their faces as they were grabbing him?'

'He says they were in an area where the streetlamp was burnt out.'

'And when he woke up?'

'He didn't see anything. He was blindfolded with a bandanna and his hands were tied behind his back. They'd even bound his feet. All he could hear was dogs and sheep. He must have been in a house in the country. Then on the fourth day they shoved the cotton over his nose again and he woke up outside Vigàta.'

'Do you believe this kidnapping story?' Montalbano asked him.

'Yes and no. As far as Borsellino is concerned, the only thing we can be really sure of is that he's dead.'

'The story doesn't make sense to me,' said Montalbano. 'Even assuming he was kidnapped.'

'I'll try to find out more,' Fazio promised.

'Explain to me why it doesn't make sense,' said Mimì.

'First of all, the manner of the kidnapping. How did the kidnappers know that Borsellino would be at the board of directors' meeting that evening? And what interest could the Cuffaros have possibly had in paying a large sum to free Borsellino? Was he a close relative of theirs? No. Until proven otherwise, he was just the manager of a super-market. And yet they paid up with no questions asked.'

'And how do you explain it?' asked Augello.

'I've thought of something. We should find out who Borsellino's wife was.'

'Already taken care of,' said Fazio.

'Well, wouldn't you know it!' the inspector yelled.

Fazio looked at him in shock.

'Never mind, I'm sorry, go on.'

'Can I take a piece of paper out of my pocket?'

'You have my authorization,' the inspector said through clenched teeth.

Fazio pulled out a folded half-sheet, opened it, and started reading.

'Caterina Fazio—'

'A relative of yours?'

'No, sir. Caterina Fazio, daughter of Paolo Fazio and Michela née Giummara, born at Ribera on 3 April 1955, married to Guido Borsellino. Died of a cardiac arrest in Vigàta on 7 June 2001.'

He folded the paper up again and put it back in his pocket.

Montalbano flew off the handle.

'What the fuck do I care about when she lived and died?! I wanted to know whether she was related to the Cuffaros!'

'No relation,' Fazio declared calmly.

'So if the Cuffaros paid a big ransom for someone who wasn't even remotely related to them, why did they do it?'

'Maybe they were fond of Borsellino,' said Mimì.

Montalbano didn't even consider this remark worthy of a glance.

'The only possible explanation is that Borsellino wasn't just a simple employee, but something more. But what? Fazio, I think it was you who told me that it was the Honourable Mongibello who got him the job at the super-market. What did he do before that?'

'He was an accountant for the Cuffaros, for certain business deals they had in . . .' The dream about that American film, the one with the scene of the capture of Al Capone, came back to him and unfolded before his eyes in all the glittering magic of CinemaScope, as the advertisements used to say. Apparently he'd had that dream because the suspicion had been lingering inside him for a long time, hidden, never coming to the surface.

'An accountant!' he howled, leaping to his feet with eyes bulging.

Fazio just looked at him, a furrow appearing in the middle of his brow.

Mimì made light of the situation.

'Calm down, Salvo! What's wrong with you? Accountants aren't some sort of endangered species. So Borsellino was an accountant. So what?'

'Mimì, you don't understand a fucking thing!'

'I understand,' said Fazio.

'Then please explain it to the senior detective inspector while I smoke a cigarette.'

He smoked it at the window, and when he'd finished, he sat back down.

'If I've understood correctly, you think Borsellino might have been the chief and only accountant for all of the Cuffaros' businesses, is that right?' Augello asked.

'It's just a hypothesis, Mimì, but it should be checked out. It would be the only explanation of why the Cuffaros paid the ransom. They couldn't risk losing someone so important to them, someone who knew all their secrets.'

'Wait a second,' Augello retorted. 'If Borsellino was so important, why did they have him killed just a few months later, going through that whole song and dance of the supermarket burglary?'

'Because apparently something had happened that made them no longer trust him,' Montalbano replied.

'But why? What reason could Borsellino have given them to doubt him?'

Augello's question was left momentarily unanswered. Then the inspector, whose brain was whirring to the point of overheating, said:

'Maybe it was because of the kidnapping itself.'

'Explain what you mean.'

'Maybe the Cuffaros reasoned the way I just did. They too must have wondered how the kidnappers managed to know that Borsellino would be attending the meeting that evening. Fazio just said that they convened exceptionally, and unexpectedly, to the point that Borsellino didn't have his papers in order. Who informed the kidnappers?'

'Someone from the board of directors?' Mimì ventured.

'I would rule that out, since by now the culprit would have already been singled out by the Cuffaros and killed. Fazio, do you know of any member of the council who was recently offed?'

'No, they're all still alive.'

'Maybe . . .' Montalbano began, then immediately stopped.

'Maybe?' Augello egged him on. But the inspector was lost in thought. Silence filled the room. And the phone took advantage and started ringing.

'Chief? 'Ere's the young lady siccritary o' Mr Mito onna line sayin' as how 'e jess got back.'

Montalbano hung up and then rose to his feet.

'Both of you come with me. We're going to the Free Channel studios in Fazio's car.'

*

'You have no idea what a nasty piece of work this La Cava is!' said Nicolò Zito. 'He's a vicious dog that won't give up his bone! There was no way I could persuade him I hadn't faked the burglary! I'm lucky I have a good lawyer, or I'd still be there now!'

'Do you have the copy of the recordings?'

'I can see you're very interested in my ordeal. Thanks. Of course I have the copy. I've kept it on me the whole time, even when I went to see the judge. I had it made for a normal tape recorder, since you would never be able to work out how to use the digital kind.'

'As far as that goes, I don't know how to use the normal kind either.'

Zito pulled a tiny cassette out of his breast pocket and handed it to him.

'Can I ask another favour of you?' Montalbano asked.

'Sure, as long as I won't end up back again in front of La Cava.'

'Can we all listen together to this recording right now?'

'I can give you about an hour. But then I have to prepare the report on Strangio's suicide. It's blockbuster news and I've got material from three different cameramen to sort out. But what's so important about that recording?'

'There's a phone conversation between Borsellino and an unknown person that took place before Augello got there. I want you to hear it too.'

Zito took a small cassette player out of a drawer, put the cassette in it, ran it backwards and forward until they heard Borsellino's voice saying:

'Hello? This is Guido.'

'That's the one,' said Montalbano, who'd read and reread the transcription.

They listened to it in silence.

'Can I hear that again?' asked Zito.

He listened to it carefully again and then said:

'It's clear that the man to whom Borsellino is reporting the burglary already knows what's happened. He gives himself away without wanting to.'

He sat there for a spell, thinking.

'You guys mind if I listen to it one more time?'

'Why?' Montalbano asked.

'I'll tell you afterwards.'

When it had finished, Zito said:

'Come with me.'

All four of them went into a room packed with video-cassettes. Zito searched around for a while, then picked one out and slipped it into a VCR beside a monitor before Montalbano stopped him.

'Nicolò,' he said, 'if you tell me you want me to listen to the voice of an honourable parliamentarian, I swear I'm going to hug and kiss you.'

'How'd you guess?' asked Zito, smiling.

Montalbano hugged him and kissed him. It was exactly what he'd been hoping for.

Ten minutes was enough to dispel any doubts anyone might have. The unknown voice on the phone to Borsellino belonged to none other than the Honourable Mongibello himself.

✻

'Do me a favour,' Montalbano said to Fazio as they were going out. 'Take Mimì back and then come and pick me up in front of Montelusa Central.'

It took him ten minutes on foot to reach the shop he was looking for.

'I'd like a mobile that doesn't cost much.'

'You've come to the right place. We're having a sale, with a ten-euro phone card prepaid.'

The salesman opened the display case, took the phone, and showed it to him.

'It costs only thirty euros.'

'OK.'

'Let me see some sort of ID,' said the salesman.

Montalbano got flustered. He didn't know you needed ID. The salesman noticed.

'You don't have an ID card?'

'I do, but I left it in the car, which is parked a long way away. Let's forget about it.'

But the salesman didn't want to lose a sale.

'Perhaps if you knew the number on your ID card . . .'

'That I do,' Montalbano improvised. 'ID card number 23456309, issued by Sicudiana Town Hall to the name of Michele Fantauzzo, Via Granet 23, Sicudiana.'

The salesman wrote down the information.

'Could you explain to me how it works?' Montalbano asked.

After getting his explanation, he paid and went out, putting the device in the left-hand pocket of his jacket. In the other he had the recorder Zito had lent him, the instructions for which he'd even written down on a piece of paper – after having them explained to him a good ten times. He started running towards Montelusa Central.

*

The first thing he did when he got home was pick up the telephone and look for a number, which he then wrote down on a piece of paper.

He went into the kitchen. Adelina had made him a salad of rice and clams, mussels, and baby octopus pieces.

For the second course, fried calamari and scampi. He laid the table on the veranda and had a feast.

Wanting to kill time until at least midnight, he sat down in the armchair and turned on the TV. There was a movie with Alberto Sordi on. He watched this for a while, then switched to TeleVigàta news. Mr Chicken-Arse Face was just finishing his editorial:

. . . it wasn't a proper letter he left, but just a note, which we've had a chance to look at, and which said only: 'My son Giovanni did not kill Mariangela Carlesimo. I did. I'd been having an affair with her for some time. We had a quarrel, and I lost my head.' These words were followed by his signature. I feel now that it is my duty to explain why we here at TeleVigàta were so long convinced of the guilt of Giovanni Strangio, the son. This young man . . .

He turned it off and went out on the veranda with whisky and cigarettes. So Michele Strangio hadn't mentioned either the phone calls or the bathrobe. He would call Fazio in the morning to tell him to get rid of it.

He felt a bit uneasy about what he had in mind to do. When the commissioner, in his office, had informed him of the president's suicide, he'd felt overwhelmed by a sense of guilt. Even though there was no question that his intention had not been to push the man to suicide, but simply to smoke him out in the hope that he would make a false move, that death had weighed heavily on him at that moment. Then it occurred to him that he might not have had anything to do with Strangio's death. It was a voice in the night, an anonymous voice, that had told him this. A voice in the night that could easily have been the voice of his conscience. The justification was a bit of a stretch, and a bit hypocritical, of course, but to a Jesuit it would have held up. Anyway, why should he have so many scruples in dealing with people who didn't even know what scruples were and did nothing but constantly escape punishment by using their political power? No, he would do what he'd decided to do. And if it worked the first time around, it would work again the second.

It was now half-past midnight. Montalbano got up, went over to the telephone, picked up his mobile, and dialled his own number. The phone started to ring. Reassured by the success of his test, he turned his attention to the recorder, keeping the instruction sheet in view. The second test also went well. Then he took the usual clothes peg out of the broom cupboard, pinched his nose with it, and dialled on his mobile the number he'd written down earlier.

'Hello, who is this?' asked the voice of the Honourable Mongibello.

Without answering, Montalbano turned on the tape, keeping the receiver right up next to the speaker. When the recording had finished, he said:

'D'ja like that? Ya wasted yer time stealin' the recorder!'

'Who's speaking? What do you want?'

'Can't figger out what I want?'

'Speak clearly.'

'When I feel like speakin' clearly, I'll letcha know.'

He hung up before the other could protest. He had a shower and then got into bed.

He slept straight through and didn't wake up until past nine.

*

'Cat, send Fazio to me, would you?' he said as he entered the office.

'I'm incatacipated, Chief, 'cause the foresaid ain't onna premisses.'

'Do you know where he went?'

'Yessir, Chief. Diss mornin' 'e come in an' 'enn 'e went straight back out, an' as 'e's passin' by me on 'is way out, 'e said as 'e's passin' by me 'at 'e was called inna the c'mishner's office.'

What could they want with Fazio at the commissioner's office?

'Is Augello in?'

'Nahssir, 'e called sayin' as how 'e's gonna be late.'

'Then get somebody to replace you and come into my office.'

'Straightaways, Chief.'

The inspector had barely sat down when Catarella came in.

'Lock the door behind you and sit down.'

257

Catarella obeyed and then stood at attention in front of Montalbano.

'I told you to sit down.'

'I can't, Chief. My legs refuse, outta rispeck f' yiz, sir.'

'Well, at ease then, otherwise I feel like I'm talking to a puppet.'

Catarella assumed the regulation 'at ease' stance.

'Everything I'm about to tell you must remain between you and me.'

Catarella teetered.

'What's wrong?'

'Jest a li'l dizzy spell, Chief.'

'You feel all right?'

'The fack 'at 'ere's gonna be a secret 'tween me an' yiz makes my 'ead spin, Chief.'

Montalbano asked him the question he had in mind. Catarella explained what he had to do. The inspector gave him some money and told him to go and buy what he needed and to take it to his house in Marinella, where Adelina was still working.

＊

Fazio checked back in at around eleven, wearing a face so gloomy that Montalbano got worried.

'What happened?'

'I was called in this morning by Vice-Commissioner Sponses.'

'Who's he?'

'He's the official in charge of Anti-terrorism.'

'God, what a pain! Do they want us to get involved in something of theirs?'

'No. But he cautioned me not to do any more work on Borsellino's kidnapping.'

Fazio, expecting a violent reaction from the inspector, was taken by surprise. Montalbano was smiling.

'Tell me exactly what he told you.'

'He said he'd found out I was going around asking questions about the kidnapping and ordered me to stop.'

'Did you ask why?'

'I certainly did. He said it was better if everyone forgot about the whole affair. He said Borsellino's suicide had prevented a certain thing from reaching its conclusion, and so the less it was talked about, the better.'

'Let me get this straight. So Sponses believes that Borsellino killed himself?'

'He seemed pretty convinced of it to me.'

'That means Sponses hasn't spoken to the commissioner. And that the order to stop investigating is an independent decision of Anti-terrorism.'

'That's the impression I had too. But now you have to explain to me why you were smiling.'

'Because I was convinced that Borsellino was kidnapped by the Anti-Mafia people, when it turns out it was Anti-terrorism. There's a considerable difference.'

Fazio looked completely bewildered.

'I haven't understood a thing.'

'It's like this, Fazio. I was convinced that the only ones who could have had any interest in kidnapping Borsellino were the Anti-Mafia people, to get their hands on his account books. But I wondered how they happened to know that Borsellino would be attending that board of directors' meeting that evening, and I had no answer.'

'But the question remains even if it was Anti-terrorism that kidnapped him!'

'No, it doesn't. That changes things. Say Borsellino finds out that one of the Cuffaros is in contact with terrorists. You can do good business with those people. Like, for example, offering them a safe base of operations. But the risk is much greater than with drug dealing or protection money or corruption. And Borsellino, in fact, gets scared about this initiative. It's one thing to do the accounts for the Mafia, and something else to be accused of complicity with terrorists. One way or another, Anti-terrorism get wind of the matter. And they start putting pressure – it's anybody's guess how – on Borsellino. Who gives in and decides to talk. But if he's going to talk, he wants his back covered. So they have to put on some kind of act. Anti-terrorism suggest they fake a kidnapping at the right moment, and Borsellino himself will tell them when it's the right moment. And as soon as he's summoned to the meeting, he informs Sponses. During those four days they talk and perhaps come to an agreement, but Borsellino asks for time so he can work out a way to let them see the compromising documents. And so they grant him time.

The best part of the whole thing is that to make the kidnapping seem real, they demand a fortune from the
Cuffaros – who at some point, however, start to suspect
Borsellino. So they kill him, making it look like a suicide
so that Anti-terrorism don't get suspicious. Sponses, without knowing it, has done us a favour. He's confirmed what
I'd been thinking.'

*

He didn't feel like eating; he was too agitated. But he still
took his customary stroll along the jetty, if only to distract
himself. At five minutes to three he went back to the office.

'Did you get everything?' he asked Catarella.

'Yeah, Chief, I wenn inna shop in Montelusa jess like
you ast, an' 'enn I took the stuff I boughted to yer 'ouse
in Marinella. Lemme go 'n' get ya the change.'

After Catarella went out, the inspector got up and
locked the door. Then he sat back down and called Montelusa Central on the outside line.

'Commissioner Sponses, please. This is Montalbano.'
To make the time go by, he reviewed the times table for
seven. When he got to seven times nine, Sponses answered
but didn't give him time to say anything.

'Listen, Montalbano, we haven't had the pleasure of
meeting, but if you're calling about that kidnapping business, I can tell you right away that—'

He was tempted to tell him to stick it you-know-
where, but he needed Sponses as much as he needed air.

'I'm calling for another reason. Think you could give me half an hour of your time?'

'Wait just a second while I check. I'm a little busy. Tomorrow morning at ten OK with you?'

'Perfect, thank you.'

He hung up and dialled another number.

'Nicolò? Montalbano here. I need a favour from you.'

'Jesus, Salvo! Have you become a professional pain in the arse or something? What do you want?'

'If I come to your office would you interview me?'

'And you'll also write down the questions I'm supposed to ask you?'

'Good guess.'

'And you probably want it broadcast on the eight-thirty report?'

'Good guess again.'

'Come at seven-fifteen sharp.'

EIGHTEEN

'Inspector Montalbano, we've invited you here to our studios in the hope that you might apply your investigative acumen to a case in which we at the Free Channel have become involved. As you and our listeners know, a few days ago we were anonymously sent a digital recorder that used to belong to Guido Borsellino, a former supermarket manager in Vigàta, which contained, among other things, recordings of conversations between Borsellino and Inspector Augello, your second-in-command, and then between Borsellino and yourself. We then broadcast these recordings. That same night, however, unknown burglars broke into our offices and stole the digital recorder — exclusively, taking nothing else. So, Inspector Montalbano, my first question is this: who would have an interest in exculpating you of the accusation that some have levelled at you, namely, that you drove the late Guido Borsellino to suicide?'

'I think the question should be put differently. Who would have an interest in giving the lie to those people who have been levelling those accusations at me and my second-in-command?'

'Does that make any difference?'

'It makes a lot of difference. Sending that recorder was not a gesture in my favour, but a hostile act towards those claiming that Borsellino was driven to suicide.'

'And who might it have been that sent us the recorder?'

'Well, let me preface that by saying that these are only my personal opinions. First and foremost, I think we are dealing with people close to Borsellino who knew that he occasionally used that recorder. I believe, however, that there is, in this affair, a sort of "fifth column" that is try-ing to exploit Borsellino's supposed suicide to their greatest advantage.'

'Why do you say "supposed" suicide?'

'Because we have strong doubts that it was really a sui-cide.'

'Can you give us some indication of why?'

'I'm sorry, but the investigation is still ongoing.'

'Let's move on to another question: why do you think the recorder was stolen from us?'

'Most probably because that recorder contained other recordings as well. And maybe one of them has proof that the presumed suicide involved persons considered above suspicion. In short, whoever sent you the recorder was not the same person who stole it from you. But, whatever the case, it was a useless, stupid move, in my opinion.'

'Why do you say that?'

'Because I am firmly convinced that whoever sent you Borsellino's recorder had copies made of all the recordings on it first; that they didn't leave themselves empty-handed. That would be typical behaviour for an extortionist.'

'*Do you think that, because of the fake suicide, someone may try to blackmail those behind it?*'

'I'd say it's quite likely.'

'*Thank you, Inspector Montalbano, for having accepted our invitation and answered our questions.*'

'Thank you.'

✻

As he was heading back down towards Vigàta he started singing out loud in the car. The interview, with all its ins and outs, the things said and not said, was certain to give the Cuffaros a few headaches. But the one it was certain to scare the most was the Honourable Mongibello, because he would realize that among the persons considered above suspicion the inspector was including him too. And so he would find himself between a rock and a hard place: on one side, there was the person who had called him on the phone and played him the recording, and on the other side, there were the police. At this very moment, he was in a cold sweat just waiting for the blackmailer's next call.

He went back to the station and locked himself in his office with Catarella.

'Explain to me again what I have to do to make the thing work.'

After the second explanation, he said:

'Maybe it's better if I write it down.'

He wrote it down on a half-sheet of paper, which he put in his jacket pocket.

Then he sped home to watch the interview.

✻

Zito performed well. He broadcast the interview at the end of the news report, after having solemnly announced it at the beginning. Montalbano was more than certain that Mongibello was watching, and that his heart must be pounding hard at that moment.

He laid the table on the veranda and treated himself to pasta 'ncasciata and swordfish, then went back inside and started looking for a good movie on TV.

He found a broadcast of *Bad Lieutenant* and watched the whole thing. At eleven-thirty he got up, took out of his pocket the instructions he'd written down at the office, read them over twice, then found the cassette player he'd got Catarella to buy for him and plugged it in.

Then he opened a little box, also bought for him by Catarella, and took out its contents, which consisted of a cord with a sort of sucker at one end and a small jack at the other. Following the instructions, he stuck the sucker onto his mobile and slipped the jack into the cassette player.

The equipment was ready now, but he had to test it to see whether it worked, and whether he'd done the right things.

He called Livia on his mobile and immediately pressed the red button with the abbreviation 'Rec' under it. 'Hi,

Livia. I'm calling you now because I have a bit of a head-ache and am going straight to bed.'

They spoke for five minutes, then wished each other a good night.

After he hung up, he pressed the rewind button, then pushed the green button. And he immediately heard his own voice. Wow! It worked! A miracle!

He went to wash his face, then came back and sat down at the table. He closed his eyes for a moment as he reviewed in his head what he had to do — all these complicated things involving recorders, video cameras, and computers were really not his forte. He got up, put the clothes peg over his nose, sat down again, and dialled Mongibello's number as he turned on the recorder.

'Hello?' said the politician, who sounded like he had his hand over the receiver.

Montalbano turned on the taped copy of the digital recording.

'*Hello? This is Guido.*'

He let it play for a few moments, then stopped it.

'Figgered out who I am?'

'Yes.'

'Wanna make a deal?'

'Yes.'

'I'll make you a reasonable offer. Two million.'

'But—'

'No buts. Two million. Tomorrow at midnight, at the old signal box in Montereale. Come alone. If I see any of your little Cuffaro friends with you, I won't come out in the open, an' I'll send the tape to the Free Channel. Leave the money outside the cabin door an' then get the hell out of there.'

'What about the tape?'

'I'll send it to you.'

'But how can I be sure that—'

'You'll just have to trust me. An' be careful. If you give me marked notes, you can consider yisself a marked man. Unnastan'?'

'Yes.'

He put down the phone, rewound the tape, and pushed the green button.

'Hello?' said Mongibello at the other end.

'*Hello? This is Guido.*'

Just to be sure, he listened to the whole recording. Not until he went to bed did he realize that he still had the clothes peg over his nose.

✲

He got to the station at eight-thirty the next morning and immediately locked himself in his office with Catarella.

'I want you to make me a copy of everything.'

'But, Chief, t'make a copy from bote tings ya need a toid recorder!'

'Do you know if there's anyone here . . . ?'

'Isspecter Augello's prolly got one.'

'Go and see.'

Catarella returned in triumph with a recorder and a new cassette. When they'd finished and Catarella was returning the recorder to Augello, Montalbano put the cassette in a drawer and locked it.

Then he headed for Montelusa at a leisurely pace.

At five minutes to ten he entered Montelusa Central through the back door to avoid running into Dr Lattes, who would certainly have mentioned the encounter to the commissioner.

He asked a guard to explain to him where Sponses's office was, then knocked on the closed door.

'Come in.'

He went in. Sponses stood up and came forward to greet him, hand extended. He was a physically fit man of about forty, with blue eyes and a decisive manner. He seemed likeable enough to the inspector.

'Please sit down. Let's get straight to the point. Why did you want to see me?'

The inspector reached into his left jacket pocket and took out the cassette recorder with the copy of the recording of Borsellino's call to Mongibello.

'There's a very brief telephone call here that I would like you to listen to carefully.'

He turned on the tape. When it was over, Sponses asked:

'Who's at the other end?'

He'd recognized Borsellino's voice perfectly well and hadn't hidden that fact. They were off to a good start.

'The man at the other end is the Honourable Mongibello, who as you must know is the president of the company—'

'That owns the supermarket, a company made up of front men for the Cuffaro family. Well, this phone call certainly presents an interesting new element. Which is that Mongibello knew about the burglary before Borsellino told him. But, even leaving aside this detail, the phone call, if anything, shows that it wasn't you or your second-in-command that drove Borsellino to suicide, but Mongibello himself, who cut him loose in brutal fashion.'

'Except that Borsellino did not commit suicide; he was hanged.'

Sponses frowned darkly.

'Do you have proof?'

'Indirect proof,' said Montalbano. 'Did you know that a local television station anonymously received a digital recorder containing—'

'I know everything.'

'Did you know that the digital recorder was stolen the night of the broadcast?'

'No, I didn't.'

'I asked myself why they did it, since the recording of my conversations with Borsellino had already been aired. The only possible answer was that there was more inside that recorder. Luckily the station manager had a copy made of everything in the recorder. And he gave it to me. And in it I found the phone call I just had you listen to. You see, Sponses, if Borsellino really had killed himself, that phone call would be of no real importance. But if Borsellino was murdered, then Mongibello, by letting it slip that he knew about the burglary, shows that he's aware of a larger plan, which is the elimination of Borsellino himself. Who was killed because the Cuffaros discovered that he was in contact with you. They were unconvinced by the kidnapping that you set up with him. They did some investigating and found some things out, so they set up the fake suicide, using his complicity in the supermarket burglary as the motive. And all this just so you wouldn't suspect that they'd discovered that Borsellino was in touch with you. Some poor nightwatchman even lost his life because of it, because he happened to be passing in front of the supermarket when the supposed burglar was going in.'

Sponses said nothing, but only got up, went over to the window, hands in his pockets, and looked outside. Then he came and sat back down.

'Listen, Montalbano. Your argument makes sense. But it's only one argument, don't you see? We would never, in a court of law, succeed in establishing Mongibello's complicity solely on the basis of that phone call.'

'Actually, I'd anticipated this observation on your part,' the inspector said.

And from his other pocket he extracted the recorder with his own phone call to Mongibello and set it down on the desk beside the first one, but before turning it on, he said:

'I have to explain first that before this call there was another one that was not recorded, in which an unknown person had Mongibello listen to a recording of his phone conversation with Borsellino, and then told him that he'd be in touch soon.'

'Wait a second,' said Sponses. 'How do you know this?'

'If you listen to the tape, it'll become clear to you.'

He turned it on. When it was finished, Sponses's face was red as a beetroot. Apparently he was shaken by what he'd just heard.

'Do you know who the blackmailer is?'

'Yes. Me.'

Sponses leapt forward in his chair as if he'd just sat on a landmine.

'But that's totally illegal!'

'Oh, yeah? And your fake kidnapping of Borsellino I suppose was completely legal? You guys fight terrorism by resorting to methods well outside the law, and you reproach me for doing something similar? Sponses, I'm offering you a golden opportunity. By agreeing to pay the ransom, Mongibello is implicitly admitting his guilt. And the fact that he hasn't reported the blackmail is further confirmation. Think about it.'

Sponses thought it over for a spell, then made up his mind.

'I can't make any decision on my own, you realize. Leave me all the materials here. I'll call you no later than three o'clock this afternoon, OK?'

'Who do you want to talk to about it?'

'With my superiors and with the prosecutor.'

'Who is it?'

'La Cava.'

You couldn't ask for more.

'You'll have to hurry. The appointment is for midnight tonight. Oh, and I should also tell you, just so you know, that I've made a copy of everything I'm leaving you here.'

'I didn't doubt it for an instant,' said Sponses.

*

Sponses's call came at three o'clock sharp. Montalbano hadn't budged from his office since returning from his meeting with him. He'd felt so nervous awaiting his reply that he hadn't even felt hungry for lunch.

'Come right away.'

He sped off in his car as never before and even raced up the steps to Sponses's office.

'Tell me everything,' he said, out of breath.

'There's good news and bad news.'

'Start with the bad.'

'La Cava isn't on board. He says he can't take a legal action based on an illegal one – your blackmail, in other words. But he gave me some good advice.'

'And what's that?'

'He said that we should both forget – that is, La Cava and I should forget – that we ever spoke about this.'

'And that seems like good advice to you?'

'Look, he didn't say we shouldn't conduct the operation. He just said he didn't want to hear about it before the fact. But if we tell him the whole story after all has been said and done – the whole story except for the blackmail part, that is – with our excuse being, say, that we didn't have enough time to tell him about it, then he'll act accordingly without asking us too many embarrassing questions.'

'I get the picture. The whole story of my blackmail has to disappear. And what's the good news?'

'My bosses have decided to go through with the operation anyway.'

'And what are you going to replace my blackmail with?'

'We're going to say a mole informed us that Mongibello was being blackmailed by an unknown person and so on. Got that?'

'Got it.'

'One last thing, maybe the worst thing for you. You're no longer operational.'

He'd been expecting this. He would have bet his balls that this was the price they would make him pay.

'So I have to stay out of it?'

'Right. As of this moment, everything passes into our hands.'

'Can you tell me why?'

'Because before you could take any action you would need to request the authorization of the prosecutor, who, since this involves a Member of Parliament, would be required to inform the undersecretary, who would be required to inform the minister . . .'

Montalbano swallowed the bitter pill.

But Sponses was right. The fewer politicians were involved in the matter, the better. They were liable to undermine all the work that had been done. 'I understand perfectly. Fine. Whatever you say.'

He got up to leave.

'Thanks for everything,' said Sponses. 'I'm glad to have met you.'

'Me too. Oh, listen, there's something I should warn you about. Mongibello will almost certainly have spoken to the Cuffaros about the blackmail. I don't think he'll come alone to the appointment. I think the Cuffaros will have decided to spring into action as soon as the blackmailer comes and picks up the money.'

'But if they kill him they won't have the tape!'

'I don't think they'll want to kill him. I think their intention will be to kidnap him and torture him until he tells them where he's hidden it.'

'Thanks for the warning.'

'Listen, would you do me a favour? Could you call me at home tonight after you've completed the operation?'

'Absolutely. Give me the number.'

*

How was he going to make the hours go by, since he wasn't the least bit hungry? After his meeting with Sponses he'd gone straight home, undressed, and plunged into the icy sea. He'd swum until he lost all strength and sense of time. Then he went back to the house and sat down on the veranda with his cigarettes and whisky within reach. There was half a bottle and he drank it all down.

Afterwards, he went inside and sat down in the armchair. He watched a spy film about which, as usual, he didn't understand a thing. After that he switched to a love story that took place in India. Halfway through the third film, which was about samurai, he fell asleep.

The ringing of the phone woke him up. He looked at his watch. Three-thirty. Shit, it was late! He ran to the phone. It was Sponses.

'Sorry to call you at this hour, but it's a big mess. Something terrible happened.'

'Meaning?'

'Well, we'd taken up our positions and saw Mongibello arrive with a briefcase in his hand. He put it down on the ground outside the signal box, and at that exact moment we heard a gunshot and Mongibello collapsed. I ran up to him as my men raced to the spot where the shot had come from. All they found was a precision rifle with an infrared sight. They'd clearly used a marksman: Mongibello died instantly.'

'Apparently the Cuffaros felt he'd become a weak link in the chain, or even a traitor, and decided to eliminate him.'

'But they still haven't got the tape!'

'What the fuck do they care about the tape? Their

name is never mentioned in it! They'll just say that it was a private matter of Mongibello's that they knew nothing about! They'll say they're shocked! So, what line are you guys going to take now?'

'Well, that's the big mess I was referring to. We had no choice but to inform the ministry. Someone called La Cava to suggest that he pass it off as a hunting accident. But La Cava retorted that he had the wrong person. He said that the dead, at least as far as he knew, were not granted parliamentary immunity, and therefore he was going to institute proceedings against unknown persons for murder. He said he was going to turn Mongibello's life inside out like a sock. He would start with trying to find out what he was doing wandering about in some godforsaken place at midnight, carrying a briefcase with two million counterfeit euros in it.'

'Counterfeit euros?!'

'Yes, though very skilfully made. I think Mongibello got them from the Cuffaros and didn't even know they were counterfeit. I think La Cava, for his part, wants to scare the living daylights out of the Cuffaros. And we're going to do our level best to help him.'

Montalbano felt himself grow jubilant at the sound of these words – despite Sponses's overuse of clichés.

'Thanks,' he said.

'Thank *you*,' said Sponses, 'and good night.'

✻

A wolflike appetite suddenly came over him. He laid the table on the veranda and went to see what was in the fridge.

Adelina had prepared two vegetarian dishes for him: an aubergine Parmigiana that practically made him faint with its fragrance, and a salad with everything in it from lettuce and passuluna olives to potatoes and cucumbers.

He sat down outside. It was a dark night, but peaceful. Far out at sea he could see a few fishing lamps.

As he put the first forkful in his mouth, Montalbano thought that, when all was said and done, things could not have gone any better.

Author's Note

This novel was written a number of years ago. Any attentive reader who notices the more or less accentuated crises of ageing, or the more or less decontextualized quarrels with Livia, and so on, should not blame it on the author but on the secret alchemy of publishers' schedules. The names of the characters, companies, situations, and places are entirely the fruit of my imagination. I need to say this so that nobody gets the wrong idea.

Notes

pages 47-8 – **Ragonese had applauded the police after the 'Mexican butchery' they'd imported to Genoa for the G8 summit in 2001.** During the G8 summit in Genoa in 2001, Italian police used heavy-handed tactics against protesters who'd come from all over Europe. Perhaps the worst incident involved raiding the youth hostel where many were sleeping, dragging them violently out of bed, inflicting serious injury on several of them, and then arresting them. Later a young man was killed when he threatened carabinieri with a dustbin during a demonstration.

page 53 – **'Congratulations on your run of luck.' / 'You can even call it by its proper name: *culo*.'** In Italian slang, *culo* (ass, arse, buttocks) means 'good luck'. It can have the negative connotation of 'undeserved luck', especially in sporting situations.

page 69 – . . . **a man who'd been a minister and Prime Minister a great many times had been found definitively** guilty of the crime of collusion with the Mafia, and yet continued to enjoy the status of senator for life? A reference to Giulio Andreotti (1919–2013), repeatedly a fixture at the head of the Italian government for many decades.

page 78 – **'Ever since your government made it legal for people to shoot at thieves.'** In one of his several terms as Prime Minister, Silvio Berlusconi, trying to emulate lax American laws concerning firearms and their use, used his parliamentary majority to break with tradition and eased national restrictions on the possession of firearms and their use, making it legal to shoot at burglars and trespassers, even when the shooter's life isn't endangered.

page 144 – **He'd once had a similar lapse of memory involving a horseshoe and had nearly lost his life over it.** This occurs in the novel *The Track of Sand* (Mantle, 2011).

page 174 – **Cillintano:** that is, Adriano Celentano (b. 1938), an Italian rocker who has been a steady fixture on the pop music scene since ca. 1960.

page 184 – **The three biggest private television stations are the personal property of the head of the majority party, and two of the state television stations are headed by men chosen personally by the head of the majority party.** This novel was written when Silvio Berlusconi was still Prime Minister.

Notes by Stephen Sartarelli